Life on Bull Creek

William V. Harding

PublishAmerica
Baltimore

First printing

PublishAmerica has allowed this work to remain exactly as the author intended, verbatim, without editorial input.

ISBN: 1-60836-576-X
PUBLISHED BY PUBLISHAMERICA, LLLP
www.publishamerica.com
Baltimore

Printed in the United States of America

Contents

Introduction 9
Bull Creek 13
The Float Trip 17
The "Almost" Damming of Bull Creek 23
Stopping Traffic in Dawson 26
Josh Stories 29
"I'm Going to Step on YOU!" 31
Vernie Culpepper Special 32
The Amazing Exploding Cow 33
Massachusetts 34
My Trusting Mama 42
Ada Street and "The Tail" 46
The Giant Car 48
Columbus 50
Mrs. Diamond and "The Woods" 55
Why You Shouldn't Jump Off Bridges 57
A Collection of Claws 61
Alligators and Caimans 64
Raymond L. Ditmar's "Snakes of the World" 68
Mama—Bipolar Normal 70
Martin Army ER 74
Granny 76
Storeowner Defends Self—Robber Killed 83

Aunt Birdee 85
The Monkey Barn 91
"Dreckly" 95
Harmony Church 98
Insanity. Just Plain Insanity. 101
Driving Mules with Bully 103
Red-Winged Blackbird Dinner 106
Armed Forces Day Downtown 108
Pulling the Snake, the Bush, and the Line 112
Phone Pranks 117
Grampa and the "Flip" 120
Mr. Dunwoody and Terry 122
Josh 125
The Maids 132
The "Quarter" 137
Burning Up the Yard 139
Maurice 144
The Bat Cave 147
Mrs. Nall 149
Libraries and Museums 151
Skateboards 154
My First Ticket 158
J.C. Pinkston's Name 160
Tree Houses 162
A Week's Worth of Switches 164
"Annie" and Uncle Jasper 166

L.J.J.J.B.B.D. Hatcher 174
The Devil Is in the Cemetery 175
Ice Cream for Lunch 178
Mrs. Santini 180
Fish Heads on the Smokehouse 184
Eatin' Possum 188
Birdee, Tom, the Black Guy, and the Dynamite 191
Daddy 194
Waylon and Madame 199
Connecticut 203
Off to the North Country 208

INTRODUCTION

I did most of my "growing up" in Georgia, living with my one full brother, Nate, and my mother, Mattie. My Mama and Daddy divorced when I was about five years old. I also had an older half-brother, Joshua (we called him "Josh") who lived with my grandparents in a small farm town fifty-five miles away. Josh was 11 years older than me and was the product of my mother's first marriage. He was also, as it would turn out, the person I was closest to of anyone in the family

I am a Southerner at heart. Always have been, always will be. I think my brother ended up more of a Northerner after he finally seemed to cave in during the first year in Maine and decided to "toe the line", as far as Daddy was concerned. He was easily Daddy's favorite. Daddy and I didn't get along too well.

I was born in 1955; so much of this takes place

during the mid-sixties. Viet Nam is going on and I am living next door to what was then the world's largest infantry school and I am the son of an Army officer to boot! I had never met most of Daddy's side of the family. On my Mama's side of the family, I knew most, if not all, of the relatives. Sane and crazy.

This is the time of Kennedy and King, Civil Rights, Moon missions, and all the other things that made the sixties so colorful and I am living "smack dab" in the middle of it. Grampa's farm is in Parrott, 55 miles away. The closest big town is Albany and Albany is where, some might argue, the Civil Rights movement started to finally gel.

My mother and her entire side of the family is Southern Baptist and this only adds to the strangeness of some of the stories. Much of what is perceived as religion in the south is really much more like superstition.

I lived in a very unusual mix of environments—military, city, and farm and country. We lived in Columbus during the week and usually went to my grandparents' farm on the weekends and to visit my very old, and odd, "Annie" (my Great Aunt Alva) who lived about an hour from the farm. For any of you who don't understand—"Annie" is how you say "Auntie" in the south.

So it was science, the Beatles and the Dave Clark Five, high-tech (even though "high-tech" didn't exist yet), and paved streets and libraries and museums during the week, and dirt roads, mule teams, and hunting, fishing, and farming on the weekends.

Oh yeah. My mother was also bipolar (even though "bipolar" wouldn't be in the vocabulary until many years later). Even though she was from a southern farming background she managed to end up with a Master's degree and, even though her parents didn't agree, she was outspoken about the equality of man. As a measure of the other side of the coin, Granny paid the "niggras", as she referred to them, 25 cents an hour until she went to the nursing home (Josh made sure that the purses of those who put up with her intolerable behavior got padded during the time he managed the farm). I truly believe that she thought that they didn't have anything else better to do.

Prior to the age of eighteen, I had lived the biggest part of my life in Georgia, except for a year in Connecticut when I was 12 and four years of high school in Maine. I had lived other places before the age of four, but those are other stories that I have little memory of.

I come from a family (mother's side) that was steeped in the oral tradition. Stories were an important part of the fabric that bound this side of my family together. So here are some of those stories and some of my own. What I tell you may not be exactly what happened, but they are told as I remember them. Some of the "handed down" stories may or may not be true. I will tell them here the way they were told to me.

BULL CREEK

Bull Creek flows through Columbus and at one point along its travel it borders the Saint Mary's Hills neighborhood where I spent the biggest part of my "formative years". As a child and young man I spent hours exploring the banks of the creek in search of snakes, turtles, toads and frogs, salamanders, and crawdads—pretty much in that order.

The creek was a constant, sort of. I had to cross a bridge over the creek every school-day morning on my way to school and then again every school-day afternoon on my way home. One afternoon, when we had been let out early, I debated with Charles whether it was possible that Kennedy was actually dead as we crossed the bridge on the way home.

The width and depth of the creek, however, was not constant and could change dramatically whenever there was significant rainfall. The creek could be downright deadly during those times. Normally, there are only a few places on my stretch of creek where it is deep enough to swim in. I could swim in pretty shallow water. Anyway, as a young man, I believed myself to be somewhat invincible and so my exploration was continued at most every opportunity.

Bull Creek was versatile as a "play" area. There was most every kind of creek environment that you would expect to see in the Deep South at some point along the creek or one or more of its many tributaries. There were muddy areas, swampy areas, pond-like areas, brook-like areas, and river-like areas, each environment lending itself to a particular mode, or type, of play.

I should probably also say that I played a lot of "Army" as a child. I was the son of any Army officer, my mother taught school on neighboring Fort Benning, and this was just about the middle of the Viet Nam war. There was rarely a day when I did not see any number of soldiers or military equipment. The point is that I would see U.S. soldiers fighting in tropical, sometimes swampy, jungles and Bull Creek provided me with an ability to play "Army" in a somewhat representative environment. One of the main reasons Fort Benning was such a big thing for training was that it was similar in terrain to parts of the Viet Nam Highlands and its swampy areas, filled with many potentially lethal reptiles, provided another similarity.

There were also lots of my favorite animals—snakes. It is probably fortunate for me that the creek had only a small population of venomous snakes when compared to the size of the population of non-venomous snakes. I probably caught several hundred snakes on the creek between the ages of six and eleven. There were only a few scattered periods when I did not have at least one pet snake and had as many as eight at the peak, some large and some small.

In many ways I believe that I may be more resistant to certain types of infections because of all the "vaccinations" I had while playing on/in the creek. Interestingly, I do not recall ever getting any form of infection that I can attribute to the creek even when I played in the creek with an open wound from some previous mischief. For that matter, there was rarely any time in my childhood when I did not have at least some form of injury. I went through band-aids by the gross as a child. In fact, if not for my early first-aid skills, I might not be writing this text.

Bull Creek was also a treasure trove for the type of kid I was. Remember, the litterbag had only just come into being during this time. I remember the first, black and white, anti-litter public service announcements. Oh yeah, PSA's were new as well. Consequently, there was a lot of open dumping along the banks of the creek in certain areas. After all, the creek was an "automatic flush" creek. Whenever the banks were swollen, all of the rubbish, up to the high water mark, was washed away. There was always more where that came from. So I had an unending supply of building materials, old car parts, as well as parts from all sorts of mechanical devices, old lawnmowers, all sorts of construction equipment, and just about anything you could imagine and some things that you couldn't.

The Float Trip

The Float Trip started when my cohort in crime for several years, Scott, and I found a large metal concrete mixing pan. This was certainly our biggest find on the creek ever! Scott and I were both small. He probably because of years of secondhand smoke and me for unknown reasons other than I was a late bloomer. We probably didn't weigh 110 pounds between us. The benefit was that we could both fit in this pan and it would still float with a reasonable amount of sideboard. I would guess that it was probably four feet by six feet by 18 inches deep. Sort of like your rear view mirror, objects in a 10 year old's eyes maybe be smaller than remembered.

We had found the pan a mile or so upstream from my neighborhood. Scott lived in a trailer park about a half a mile further distant. We could have floated it downstream closer to home, but it was easier to hide it where it was and the creek was more pond-like at that location so we could float around while trying to figure out what to do with our newfound treasure.

We found it on a weekday, and by the time Saturday came around, it was time to do something with it. We headed down to the hiding place and got in the pan with one long stick each for pushing our boat along where necessary, as well as for holding down the head of a snake to catch it, should one be located. With a gentle push, we were off. We really had no idea of where the creek actually went beyond a roughly three-mile stretch of the creek.

The first day we made our way down through all of the area that we knew so well, pointing out places along the way where some event had occurred—where I had caught a snake, where I had almost caught a snake, where we had found a dead cat, where someone had gotten hurt.

The trip was undertaken in the summer and the creek was pretty low. We had to get out and let the pan float along beside us at some spots. Consequently, the trip progressed at a gentle pace leaving ample time to survey the surrounding area.

By the time we got to the “school” bridge it was getting late and Scott had to get home. We hid the pan and agreed to meet back at the pan the next day. Scott's family was pretty "godless" so he didn't have to go to church Sunday morning. I wasn't as lucky, as my mother believed that going to church was as important, if not more so, than going to school. My mother's master's thesis was titled something like "The Contribution of Sunday Schools in Primary Education", or something like that.

After getting home from church I grabbed a bologna sandwich and was off. You have to understand that we couldn't take our bikes because we weren't going to be coming back that day and the chances of the bikes getting stolen was far greater than the pan getting stolen.

We finally met up around 12:30 and were off down the creek again.

Remember when I said that we knew a certain length of the creek? Also, remember that at this point, I was ten, and so maps were not something that I used very often. Well, as it turns out, Bull Creek above the "school" bridge only somewhat resembles Bull Creek below the "school" bridge. For one thing, it gets a lot narrower and quite a bit deeper. There is also more industry along the creek and more trash. For us this was all the better. It was also much less work since there was so much depth and flow that it was sort of like watching a movie as we floated down the creek. It was too deep to reach the bottom with the sticks and we didn't have paddles (we hadn't ever needed them before) so we were pretty well limited as far as the ability to stop. We didn't care. We hadn't really considered the possibilities.

With more trash, there were more rats. Something we saw only occasionally up stream. They were just other animals to us. If we had known anything about a rat's ability to swim, we might have been a little more concerned. My mother would have probably passed out, but she wasn't there.

We were able to stop at a few points along the way and climb up the banks to survey our location. Fortunately, for us, Bull Creek flows towards Fort Benning, so I was familiar with the places along the way well enough to tell how far we were from home with some degree of accuracy. Or at least how far we were from home as accurately as I could at ten.

Late in the afternoon of the second day we finally gave in and aborted the mission. I also knew that I was probably in trouble. Scott's folks didn't care as long as they didn't get a visit by the Police.

Trying to save the "boat" was out of the question since we would probably never make it this far down the creek ever again. We were pretty sure that would be forbidden once we got home. What to do? We finally settled on setting it “free”. We put our sticks in the pan and sent it on down the creek. We put the sticks in because we figured whoever got it next might need them. We watched the pan until it disappeared around the next bend and then headed back to “civilization”.

Back then, people would let you use their phone, and so Scott and I headed for the nearest open business we could find. Even though there were many businesses near where we got off the creek, this is also the South, and back then, so-called “Blue” laws prohibited the conduct of many kinds of business on Sunday.

When we finally found a phone, I called Mama and said we needed a ride. She asked where I was and when I told her, I thought she was going to faint—Scott and I had traveled several miles from home which would have been a respectable distance in a canoe, let alone a cement mixing pan.

Mama picked us up and we were probably spared a harsher treatment because she was so happy we were OK. Also, since she didn’t know what we had done until it was over, it was better than if she had been sitting around worried, waiting for us, or the

Police, to call. Needless to say, it was pointed out to us that we had done something very dangerous and were not to repeat the journey again. Fat chance! Where would we get, I mean borrow, another cement mixing pan?

The "Almost" Damming of Bull Creek

Around the same time as the float trip, Scott and I were upstream from my school at a deep, slow moving bend in the creek. There was a construction company not too far from the bend up on Buena Vista Rd. By the way, in Columbus it is "Byou na" Vista and not "Bwain na" Vista.

At any rate, Scott and I were looking for snakes when we heard the bulldozer coming. Naturally, we took cover. After all, playing "Army" is more than a game—it's a lifestyle. We watched in horror as the operator slowly and methodically dammed our creek!

The operator started from one side by forming a small peninsula. He continued backing to the bank, scraping out a blade full of clay and sand; then, pushing the load forward out to the end of the peninsula. He extended the peninsula farther and farther, until the creek was dammed. The creek was probably 40'-50' wide at this point. To this day, and even with my engineering background, I have no clue as to why he did this. He did build a berm that was several feet higher than the surface of the creek but there was no way that this dam would hold and, in fact, wasn't going to last but a few minutes. The only problem for Scott and me was that we didn't know this. Give us a break! We were ten.

Scott and I quickly determined that we had to do something to save our beloved creek. We waited for the bulldozer to exit the area and then headed for the lowest point on the dam and began to dig, with our hands, a trench across the peninsula.

One thing that I did understand at ten was the erosive power of water. One of the neatest discoveries of my childhood was figuring out how to dig a hole, quickly, with a water hose with a nozzle. I knew that all we had to do was get a small flow breaching the dam, and the creek would take care of the rest.

Starting from the upstream side, the creek had risen to the bottom of the trench by the time we made it to the downstream side. The dam was quickly eroded away and within less than a day there was no indication that the dam had ever even been there. I thought to myself "You know years from now you'll be able to say that, without Scott and yourself, there wouldn't be a Bull Creek! Child Conservationists! The Guys That Saved Bull Creek!

Funny stuff. It's like that when you're ten.

Stopping Traffic in Dawson

When I was four, before my parents divorced, we were living in Dawson. Dawson was, at the time, the "Spanish Peanut Capital of the World". It was the home of the Cinderella Peanut Butter Company. Cinderella made all of the peanut butter used in the U.S. Army's C-Rations. This was the end of the Korean War and the Army bought a lot of C-Rations. Later, as a grade school kid, I ate a lot of C-Rations. We could get them at the PX on Fort Benning. They were really horrible, unless you're a kid—then they were great!

Dawson is also the closest town to Grampa's farm, which was in Parrott. That is a whole other story.

Anyway, Daddy was gone to Korea, so we moved to Dawson so my mother would be near the farm while Daddy was "overseas". I lived there with Nate and Josh in a small brick house six or seven blocks from downtown.

Josh was going to Dawson High. I am pretty sure it is still there, but since desegregation all of the white folks in the county had pulled their kids out of Public School and formed Terrell Academy. If you are white in Terrell County and have a child, they will figure out a way for your child to go to Terrell Academy. Rebates, scholarships, whatever—they will make it happen. So the public schools are filled with pretty much minority students. Or so I was told.

Anyway, Josh was a crossing guard at Dawson High. But what is more important, he had a crossing guards' helmet and belt. What a belt! It was white and was a belt with a strap that went from the belt, behind, up and over the shoulder, and down the front to the belt again. But more important, it had a SILVER BADGE! On the badge it said "CROSSING GUARD." Oh yeah, there was a whistle too!

So, when Josh was away, my brother and I would put on the "uniform", him with the helmet and me with the belt, or vice versa. Now, the problem was that we didn't have it clear about just what it was that we were supposed to do as crossing guards. Herein lies the snag. See, we knew how to stop the cars. That was easy, you put up your hand and blow the whistle and the cars stop. Imagine the power! To be four and be able to control CARS! Unfortunately, we hadn't gotten it straight about how you get the cars going again, or if that was even part of the job.

So there we were, out in the street in front of the house being self-appointed crossing guards. Fortunately, our street was not a major thoroughfare. Mama came out when she heard the cars honking their horns. As Mama told it, my brother had one side of the street, holding cars coming one way, and I had the other side, holding cars coming the other way. Mama said we had several cars in both directions. Cool! Unfortunately, it was not "cool" with Mama. What can I say? I was four.

Josh Stories

While Josh was going to Dawson High, he began, in my opinion, exhibiting signs of a desperate need to be accepted and not be an exception. Josh's father took off after a year or so. From best I can tell, it would have been, maybe, the second, or third, depressive phase of my mother's bipolar cycling from ecstasy to the pits of depression. Manic-depressives sometimes exhibit a sort of hyper-sexuality during their manic phase and, best as I can tell; my mother was probably a pretty energetic lover as a young woman, and a sort of super woman when she was in the manic phase of her bipolar cycling.

Josh was probably more sensitive to being a divorce kid than anyone could have imagined. All of his high school friends were from stable (appearing) farm families. He heard in church how divorce was bad. Most of his friends, unlike him, were of average ability.

Josh's abilities far exceeded most anyone who ever came out of that environment. He was a gifted artist and designer. He had been doing it since he was a small child when Grampa gave him a small can of red paint and a small can of blue paint and told him that all he had to do was round up the "stick" armies and dip half in red and half in blue and he would have two clearly distinguishable armies. All he had to do was be able to see it! In much the same way Frank Lloyd Wright's parents had given him blocks to play with. Josh's toys were just one-step more primitive.

Josh's grades started to fall off. As it turned out he had written something in an English class and it had been singled out as extraordinary. Wrong label! His friends started kidding him about being so smart. At the same time he started sabotaging his own work.

Mama, who was a schoolteacher, knew her son's abilities and told Josh that she was going to go and see the teacher and sort this out! He pleaded with her to not go and see the teacher and agreed that he would raise his grades. He did…but probably never to the level that they could have been.

"I'm Going to Step on YOU!"

Josh's best friend was James. James was huge! At least to my four year old self. Actually, James was just tall. Josh was small. I am several inches taller and at least 50 pounds heavier that Josh was as an adult. James was probably six feet tall as a fifteen year old. James used to come into the house and he would lift his foot high in the air, above my head and say "I'm Going to Step On You!"

At some point I apparently decided I had had enough and I stomped into the kitchen, through one of those old spring-loaded kitchen doors that opens either way, and told Mama that "James says he's going to step on me! Well, I'm going to step on him!

I was, maybe, three feet tall.

VERNIE CULPEPPER SPECIAL

Vernie Culpepper was a less well-to-do friend of Josh's. Money didn't matter much to Josh. Things were pretty rough out at the Culpepper place. Vernie's favorite food was a peanut butter and jelly sandwich, but a special peanut butter and jelly sandwich.

Like I said, things were pretty tight on the Culpepper farm and so a highpoint for Vernie was a peanut butter and jelly sandwich where the peanut butter and jelly were pre-mixed, producing an oddly gray-looking mass. But, it tastes great!

Imagine yourself dirt poor and make yourself one and maybe you'll understand.

The Amazing Exploding Cow

While we were living in Dawson, and Josh was hanging out at the Thompson farm most of the time, they had a cow that had gotten loose and got into the dried corn and dried beans and had ate its fill and then, since it was free to roam, headed down to the creek. The cow drank its fill and then probably didn't feel very well. Cows can't throw up like you and I can. So, several hours later the cow literally exploded from the internal pressure caused by the expanding corn and beans.

Mama would not let me go and see the cow no matter how much I pleaded. In the end it may be that the picture in my mind is much worse that it actually was. The picture I have in my mind is probably more of the cow that swallowed the hand grenade than the cow that ate the dried corn and beans and then drank it's fill of water.

MASSACHUSETTS

After Daddy returned from Korea, he determined that it was time to head back to New England where he was from. So off we went to Littleton, Massachusetts.

Littleton wasn't a bad place, but it wasn't a great place either. It is my first memories of "Felix the Cat" cartoons. It is my earliest memory of my mother lying on the floor, with a spilled pan of spaghetti all around, crying, making what, years later, I would know as the sound of the depressive phase of the bipolar cycle.

The few memories I have of Littleton are mostly of a single winter, and snow, and Daddy bringing the truck company by the house, and leaving.

Littleton is my first memory of snow. As I would later learn, while living in Connecticut, Massachusetts, Connecticut, and Rhode Island are only "sort of" New England compared to the rest with their fearsome winters. In Massachusetts you get a good snow a couple of times a season and the snow, many times, melts off in only a day or two and you are left with soggy yards of dead grass and lots of mud.

I remember it snowing twice while we were in Littleton. The first time was the first time I ever rode on a snow sled, and if I remember correctly I ended up getting hit by one of the other sledders.

The second time it snowed was the night before Mama and my brother and I left.

The day Daddy brought "work" home was probably in the fall or spring because I remember that it was neither hot, nor cold. Daddy pulls up in front of the house in his command Jeep with about fifty large military trucks and transport vehicles from the Army truck company that he commanded.

He had his follower Jeep come up from the rear, pick up my brother, and take him back to the rear position. Then they got out the Walkie-Talkies and let my brother and I talk to each other, he at the back of the formation and me at the front. Just so you understand, these things were the huge Walkie-Talkies you see sometimes in World War II movies or on the TV show "MASH". You wouldn't really call them portable so much as, maybe, luggable.

To his credit, Daddy did make a couple of other gestures toward my brother and me to try and "Be a Dad". One day he took us to wherever he was stationed (one of the few postings he had that I don't remember the name of) and we got to fire a .50 caliber machine gun. Not many four year olds get to shoot a big machine gun.

Daddy also made sure I got to the Corpsman when I was jumping on the bed one night and split my head open. My brother and I were both bouncing on our bunk beds that had recently been taken down and placed side by side. Now bunk beds have substantial headboards and footboards to hold one bed atop the other. We were bouncing and "BOOM!" I glanced off the footboard of my bed splitting my brow above my right eye. It was about six stitches' worth, and I got my first introduction to the Corpsmen (i.e., Medics) who would later repair me at military bases in Georgia, Connecticut, Maine, and Texas.

I remember that Mama, my brother, and I left early in the morning after Daddy had left for work, or maybe he was off on assignment. He had been spending some time at Fort Drum in Upstate New York. Anyway, it had snowed the night before and the landscape was a sculpted white, not a sharp edge in sight except for those of the houses and even some of them were rounded by the drifts.

Mama had arranged for the preacher to come, pick us up, and take us to the nearest train station.

It seemed like we were on that train for days and we probably were on it for at least two days. Along the way we met a few folks with whom Mama was very friendly, but I only remember two and I don't so much remember them as I remember what they did for me.

Mama had apparently taken my brother to the restroom, because I was alone. The seats on the train had these spring-loaded, folding footrests and if I hung off the seat, supporting myself by my elbows, I could just reach the footrest with my toes. Unfortunately, for me, I had not begun my quest for knowledge of mechanical things, and had no idea how these things worked. I only knew that I could touch it and that in itself was an accomplishment to me.

Somewhere along the way I put pressure on some part of the linkage that I would quickly wish I had not done. WHAP! Like a large, human-sized mousetrap, the footrest snapped shut with my ankles tightly in its grasp. The motion snatched me off the seat in the blink of an eye and, Boom!, I hit the floor.

AAAAAAAAaaaaaaaaHHHHHHHHHH!!!!!!!!!!!!!!

I was caught and IT HURT!

Responding to the emergency came two women in long black robes with crosses hanging from chains about their necks. Oh No! Nuns! Catholics!

I didn't know what Catholics were except that I knew that we didn't believe what they believed and these oddly dressed women, I think they were women—I couldn't really tell, had something to do with it.

The nuns released my ankles from the trap and got me back up on the seat. I didn't care if they were from Mars, they were O.K. by me. Mama arrived shortly and became immediately agitated when she saw me with the nuns—not that she had any problems with nuns (remember, Mama believes that all are equal), but the fact that they were there could only mean I had done something, hopefully not something requiring stitches.

The nuns calmed Mama down and explained what they had found and what they had done. Mama thanked them continuously for the next hour or so. They were instantly the best friends of the family. The nuns watched out for my brother and me for as far south as they went, and there were no further incidents. I am sure Mama was grateful.

Mama gave the nuns our address and my brother and I had asked if we could have crucifixes—not that we were "Hooked on Catholicism", but because they were neat models. They were 3D, instead of pictures, they were neat, in our opinion, and we didn't really have any opinions about one religion over another. About all we knew was that in our religion, you got to go for a dunk in the small swimming pool in the front of the church, behind the pulpit, when you got to be a certain age, or something like that. We also knew that there was an unspoken understanding that our's was the "right" religion.

Several weeks later, after we had settled in on the farm, a small package arrived addressed to my brother and me. We were called to what was used as the living room on the farm and given the package. To prevent us from destroying the contents in the opening process, Grampa lent us a hand and opened one end of the package. He handed the package back to us and when we retrieved the contents we found two crucifixes. One, the one that I wanted and ended up with, had a black cross that was made of plastic and having beams that were probably ¼ inch square. It was maybe three inches long. Christ was cast in off-white plastic and resembled ivory. The other crucifix was much less elaborate, but as it would turn out, much more durable.

The other crucifix had a flat, light blue cross that was probably around 1/8 inch thick with somewhat ornate scrollwork around the outer perimeter of the cross. Christ was done as a silver metal stamping, or casting, I don't remember for sure. It was fairly light construction and the Christ was riveted to the cross. In the end, this one outlasted the one that I got by years, but in all fairness, the life of my crucifix was significantly shortened after I made several attempts to "take Christ down from the cross". The other crucifix probably lasted so long because we didn't play with it and I didn't know anything about metal working at that point.

The only thing better than getting the crucifixes was Granny's reaction. Here we are bringing Catholic stuff into her Southern Baptist house and not falling on our knees and begging God's forgiveness for this blasphemous action. It was weird—to us they were just some neat toys that just so happened to include Jesus, whom we were supposed to love anyway, so what gives? After all they had cardboard hand fans from the local funeral parlor in the pews at church that had the same image.

Mama put the crucifixes away and Granny calmed down. Mama gave them back to us after we got back to Columbus, but we were not to take them with us to the farm. Ever.

My Trusting Mama

Despite the fact that my mother never thought that her faith in God was strong enough, she displayed more faith than any person I have ever known. Throughout her dealing, or not dealing, with her bipolar disorder, both before and after she was finally correctly diagnosed, she always believed that if she just prayed enough, or worshipped enough, or helped others less fortunate enough, that God would heal her.

Hyper-religion is not uncommon in manic-depressives and my mother was definitely hyper-religious during many manic periods. What do you expect? Here my mother is, in the pit of depression, and all of a sudden the brain chemicals swing and BOOM! You almost instantaneously swing from the pit of Hell to base camp on Everest and you are feeling better by the minute. Once, when my mother and I were living together toward the end of her life,

I saw my mother go from subterranean to stratospheric in an eight-hour period with no change in medication. It was just time to swing to the other end of the spectrum.

Her simple trust in God caused me many hours of worry because when I brought her to North Central Texas she refused to give up her trusting, Southern farm town ways. You will see what I mean as we go along.

Now, toward the end of her life while she could still walk, shopping was mother's main source of social interaction, besides church on Sunday, morning and evening services, and Prayer Meeting on Wednesday night. A standard Baptist church schedule. On many days, she would make the trip to the local grocery store two or three times.

She would go to the grocery store in the morning and buy some insignificant thing that she probably didn't need. Later, she might make a trip to the drug store located in the same shopping center.

After a short rest she would many times make one more trip to the grocery store. That was fine. I had no problem with any of this.

Unfortunately, mother's boldness would grow as she swung into the manic phase of her illness. During these times, she would provide a classic example of what she called "your eyes being too big for your stomach".

When I was a child we would go out to eat at Morrison's, and my brother, or me, or both, would get more food from the buffet than we could eat. At this point we got to hear about the "starving children in Africa that would give anything to have what we had on our plate that we weren't eating!"

"Your eyes being too big for your stomach shopping" means that you buy far more than you can possibly carry home, ½ mile away.

On these excursions mother would go to the grocery store, get herself a cart, and hit the shopping hard. She would do this in spite of my pleading with her to use one of the hand baskets and that way she wouldn't end up buying more than she could carry because when the hand basket got heavy she would know that she was at her carry limit. Or she could just wait until I got home and say "I would like to go to the store" and I could take her.

And load that cart up she would! In the end she would head out of the store with eight to ten plastic bags full of groceries. On several occasions she took rides with strangers that stopped to offer her a lift. This scared me to death and I tried to get her to understand that she was not on the farm any longer and that she was now in the big city and she shouldn't be doing this sort of thing.

I asked her what she had taught her students when she was teaching school and she said that she had told them not to take rides with strangers, to which I said "And..." and she said that that was for them and she was a lot smarter than those children.

AAAAAAAAAAaaaaaaaaaaaahhhhhhhhh!!!!!!!

She never stopped. She continued to make this trek whenever her mania was around to give her the boost required to undertake such an operation. She never gave up her basic faith in the goodness of mankind and her faith in God to protect her, regardless of any evidence to the contrary.

Ada Street and "The Tail"

When I was five we ended up in a tiny little one bedroom (what would now be called an "efficiency") duplex (before there were duplexes) on a dead end street named Ada Street.

Ada Street was actually an older house that had been split down the middle to form two separate units. Fortunately, early Georgia farmhouses have a lot of symmetry in many cases and this symmetry allowed the house to be "cleaved" equally in two.

Anyway, at some point during the short time we lived there, I went into the bathroom, lifted the seat (my mother raised gentlemen), and beheld a TAIL in the toilet! A TAIL! A TAIL! AND IT WAS MOVING! MAMA!

Mama determined that it was a rat and that it was sitting with its head in the P-Trap part of the toilet so it could breathe. Remember, science. Whatever Mama came up with, it still had to make sense! Then Mama did something that sounded good at the time, but I doubt if it was very effective at doing anything except making it smell so bad that the rat couldn't stand it and left. Mama determined that Lysol, as in many other instances, was the weapon of choice. She armed herself with a twisted-up wire coat hanger, with which she had tried to prod the rat away, and a large bottle of Lysol. Holding her young, scientist child behind her she poured a large quantity of Lysol into the toilet bowl and flushed the toilet. Lysol was brown at the time and it took a few seconds for the cloud to clear, but when it did, the tail was gone. Truth be known, the flush is probably what did it.

There was cheering and I believe that we celebrated with something new—TV Dinners! Only we didn't have a TV, but we did have what were called "TV Tables". These simple, folding wonders were intended to be set up in front of the seat so that one could eat a TV dinner *and* watch TV at the same time. Will wonders never cease!

THE GIANT CAR

Mama's first car was one that Grampa agreed to let her buy on her own. My brother and I were still staying on the farm while mother got things sorted out in Columbus at the new house. She had gotten a job with the Army, teaching elementary school on Fort Benning. She was staying with a friend, starting the first job in her independence from my Daddy. Unfortunately, Mama was Mama.

Mama showed up at the farm in an "I Don't Know What", huge, bulbous, enormous car. It was some huge 40's four-door. It was HUGE! It was also junk!

We got to ride in it only once or twice before Grampa intervened. Grampa was kind; it was never like him to say "I told you so!", even though he had plenty of opportunities. He took the car, gave mother back her money, which she used to follow Grampa's advice, and bought our first new car. No doubt, it probably added years to Grampa's life not having to worry about her having her car break down.

Columbus

Mama got a job teaching school on Fort Benning at Edward A. White School. First grade and remedial reading. Heaven on a Biscuit for Mama! And, since my brother and I were officer's kids we could take Mama anywhere on "Post". Specifically, we could get cheaper prices on groceries on Post.

After Ada Street, Grampa told her that she needed to buy a house. She bought a new, small, two-bedroom house in a new development in Columbus, out toward Fort Benning, called Saint Mary's Hills. It wasn't too far from "Main Post", where everything was, like the Post Exchange, or PX, as opposed to just "Post", which was everything else.

We moved into the new house one afternoon after returning from Parrott with a trunk full of Saint Augustine grass sprigs and six small pine tree seedlings when it was pouring rain. The yard was red clay and mud, no grass, nothing. Mama, my brother, and I sprigged the whole front yard with Saint Augustine and planted the six pine trees before we even went into the house. Mama said that Grampa had said that we need to do this first—but, I'm not sure that he meant "first" literally.

Behind the house was an old growth pine forest. Perfect!

Columbus was a community that was just beginning to blossom with the input from the U.S. Army's budget resources. It was directly adjacent to Fort Benning and, in fact, Fort Benning actually sort of wraps around Columbus. Columbus is the home of many notable things, places, and events. Royal Crown Cola used to be headquartered here (I don't know if they are still there, or not). Tom's, a candy and snack maker, used to be headquartered here even though the owner/inventor had been "exiled" from Georgia years before, for political reasons, or so I was told on a school field trip where we went to the candy factory. If you have ever been in a grocery store or a convenience store in the Deep South you have almost certainly seen their products.

Columbus was big enough to have a community college, one of the first shopping malls "in the tri-county area", and an airport. We had TWO TV stations! TWO!

I used to watch "Miss Pamela's Playhouse" in the morning. It was a mix of live programming and cartoons—Looney Toons, in particular.

Years later I was told that Miss Pamela got busted in a high-dollar call girl sting in downtown Columbus. Miss Pamela never did children's programming ever again. What a loss. She was as hot as Laura on The Dick Van Dyke Show. It's weird what's "hot" when you're six.

Another Columbus celebrity was Cap'n Skip, a sort of "Skipper" from "Gilligan's Island", but without Gilligan, the Professor, Mary Ann, and the rest. Cap'n Skip had a Saturday morning TV show that was sponsored by Black Cow suckers. Black Cow suckers are sort of like a Sugar Daddy sucker (caramel on a stick) covered in a chocolate coating. Cap'n Skip faded after a few years, but was then reborn as Major McCharley, who was later one of the school bus drivers when I was in the 8th grade.

One year while my brother was in the Cub Scouts (we were six and seven, or seven and eight) he was supposed to be on the Cap'n Skip show with his Cub Scout Troop. I had had oral surgery the day before where they had removed a molar that they had to cut and break into three pieces in order to get it out. I bled a lot for a couple of days.

Josh was home from Auburn on some sort of break and was staying with me while mother took my brother to the TV station for the show. Josh dialed in the TV to the appropriate channel at the appropriate time and we watched the Cap'n Skip show.

There he was, just to the right of the screen with his Cub Scout uniform and everything. I was bleeding, but I was watching.

There is a young black kid on the left, closest to Cap'n Skip when he makes his entrance. Cap'n Skip notices the kid and stops and asks him "What's so funny little boy?"

"I c-ain't tell yaaaaaa!" said the kid.

Cap'n Skip, not to be undone, asks again, "Aww! Come on. Tell me what's so funny!"

"I c-ain't tell yaaaaaa!" said the kid.

Cap'n Skip says "Aww! Come on. I'll give you a Black Cow sucker!"

"Naw, I c-ain't tell yaaaaaa!" said the kid.

Cap'n Skip says "Aww! Come on now. I'll give you two Black Cow suckers!"

"I c-ain't tell yaaaaaa!" said the kid.

Cap'n Skip says "Aww! Come on. If you tell me I'll give you a whole box of Black Cow suckers!"

"Awwl right", he said, "Aaaar-tha Lee, he faaarted!"

The place exploded. Josh and I laughed so hard that he couldn't move and I bled like a stuck pig. But we survived.

Mrs. Diamond and "The Woods"

The forest, or "The Woods", behind our house lasted for most of my childhood. This was a stretch of pine forest that was where the "By-Pass" is today. The forest extended several miles and was where my brother and I, along with Corey, Chick, and Mary Frankel spent much of our time. And, like any other mythical forest, it had to have lore, and tales, and such. And it did!

Mrs. Diamond was supposed to be an old hag who lived in a huge house on the other side of the forest. God only knows what she was really like! Or if she really existed at all! But the fact remained that she was real to us and that she owned the forest and would like nothing better than to skin the hides of a bunch of hooligans as we weren't. For all I know she was a dear, sweet woman, which is more likely the case than the former description.

Notwithstanding, she was, and remained, very real to all of us through our grammar school years, until they started work on “The By-Pass” and we saw that there really was an ”other side” and it was just more of the same—no big house, no evil Mrs. Diamond.

It was a real let down.

Why You Shouldn't Jump Off Bridges

When I was around six, I started taking charge of my own first aid needs. Mama had mixed feelings about this. On the one hand, she didn't have to worry so much about me getting hurt when she wasn't around. On the other, because I bandaged myself, she would sometimes miss noticing that I had gotten injured. I think she was just afraid that I would develop some sort of infection and it would be too late by the time she found out about the injury.

I could bandage a wound. I knew about sterilization and antiseptics and salves, some of which sound like witchcraft, but they work. Do you know why you should keep some tobacco in your medicine cabinet? Ever heard of a salve called "Icthamol"? And if you have, do you know what it is used for?

My neighborhood was crossed by one of the tributaries of Bull Creek. So there were several bridges in the neighborhood and everybody knows that if you are looking for snakes, in the summer, in the middle of the day, they will be under the bridge!

One day while pedaling my bicycle across the bridge at the bottom of the hill that we live on, I spotted a small, brown water snake. WHOA! I skidded to a stop, threw down my bicycle, and then vaulted over the side of the bridge. The bridge was probably only four or five feet above the creek bed, but when you are four feet tall that is as tall as you are, and a hefty drop.

When I hit the bottom of the creek bed, I landed in about three inches of water. I also landed on the bottom of a broken off soft drink bottle. Right up through my heel! I howled! Then I took control of my situation and determined that I was bleeding pretty badly after I removed the cola bottle fragment from my heel. I had seen actors "die" from bleeding to death in countless battle movies, and the "Daniel Boone" and "Bonanza" TV shows. I also knew that the kid at the bottom of the hill's father was a Medic, so I climbed out of the creek bed and walked, carefully, to the house that was about 30 yards away.

It was almost surreal. This kid's father answered the door (the Army had weird hours during Viet Nam) and I calmly explained my predicament, which seemed to catch him off guard, after which he looked at me and said "Huh?" He looked at me, blinked a couple of times, looked down at my "leaking" foot and said "O.K., come on in". I may have told him that I was an officer's kid. I don't remember. I did eventually learn that this could be key information.

The Medic took me into his bathroom and had me sit on the side with my feet in the tub. He flushed the wound, and scrubbed it with Betadine. He bandaged my foot and called my mother. She came and collected me. One more catastrophe averted. One more trip to Martin Army Hospital for one more tetanus shot, something that I got a lot of in my youth. Years later a doctor in Maine told me that I had had enough tetanus shots to last me for a lifetime.

I wish I could have talked to the Medic later about what his perceptions were. It must have been pretty strange to have an eight-year-old approach you, so matter of factly, about an injury. Especially one as serious as this one was. I had learned by imitation.

If I was going to be a scientist then I needed to act like one.

A Collection of Claws

My brother is, in many ways, the exact opposite of me. We have almost nothing in common, and probably disagree with each other on almost every point, and if we don't, one of us would probably step up and disagree with the other on principle alone.

Anyway, when I was around eight, I was seriously into crawdads. "Crayfish" for those of you who aren't from the South. Not little wimpy crawdads, but crawdads that were the size of small lobsters (at least when you're four feet tall). I had LOTS of crawdads and added to the collection living in a large washtub daily.

Crawdads in Georgia are pretty aggressive crustaceans. Georgia has a whole collection of wildlife that preys on the lowly crawdad. Skunks, possums, raccoons, fish, assorted waterfowl, turtles, and many other species. At any rate, there were often leftover claws from past crawdad battles that littered the bottom of the washtub. Well, my brother decided that here was something he could collect. They couldn't pinch him since they were no longer attached to the crawdad—he was in control!

The problem was that he never took into account that the claws were full of meat, and we were in the South, and in the South we have ants...see where this is going?

The biggest problem was where he kept the claws.

We had bunk beds that were split into two separate beds. As part of the sturdy construction of these beds, there were bookcases built into the headboards that spanned the width of the bed. He was using one side of the bookcases in his headboard as his display space for his claw collection, all just inches from his head.

One night, in the middle of the night, the ants finished dinner, having carted off, or consumed, all of the flesh in the claws. Oddly enough, the claw meat apparently never had a chance to putrefy. The ants were so quick that they made off with the meat before it could rot. Then they went after him!

I was awakened to the sound of him screaming! Mama ran in—"What's wrong?! What's wrong?!" In some ways it was fortunate that he had been bitten by ants in the past because that way he could at least tell Mama and me what was wrong. The ants were all over his head.

Mama rushed him off to the bathroom to try and rinse off the ants while I identified the source of the infestation and took measures. He survived, but I think he came away with a much more puzzled view of nature. He never got it.

Later, when we were older, we were back on the farm to bury my mother, and we had gone down to one of the family ponds to look around, and we spotted a large jackrabbit (something that was rare to non-existent in this area when I was a child, as were armadillos). I later learned that my brother, riding in the other vehicle, had identified the jackrabbit as a fawn. He also identified a turtle carapace/skeleton, lying belly-up, as the skeleton of an armadillo.

Alligators and Caimans

When I was around seven years old, a man moved in next-door who changed my life forever. This man was a herpetologist—a snake guy. I was in heaven and learned that there was a whole branch of biology devoted just to my favorite animal.

This man had made a life out of snakes—sweet! But the thing that this man did for me, that was probably the most important thing that he did for me, was to loan me his copy of Raymond L. Ditmar's book on snakes. I believe it was called "Snakes of the World" or something like that. That was the start of my non-fiction reading that would continue on into my adulthood. I studied the text. I memorized scale color patterns. I studied snakes and other reptiles from around the world. I came up with my favorite—the Anaconda. But, since I couldn't have an anaconda, I settled on the South American Caiman. Alligators were in serious decline and headed for the endangered species list, but you could still buy a caiman in the pet department at the local Five and Dime.

After much pleading with Mama I got her to buy me a caiman for an early birthday present one year. By the way, there were always early birthday presents where we had promised Mama that she didn't have to get us anything for our birthdays if she would just let us have the early birthday present. It was horrible of us who knew full well that we weren't going to see a birthday where we didn't get anything!

I brought the caiman home and chained it in a boggy part of the uphill side of the yard and there he lived for about a year until a bad storm hit and his moorings washed away and off he went. I have often wondered what happened to that caiman. Given the terrain, it is likely that he made it to the Chattahoochee and out of the state, or at least out of town. Columbus has had plenty of experience with alligators and caimans. When I was eleven, a group of kids had been playing with a piece of chain, throwing it into a storm drain and then pulling it back out. On what was to be the final throw, the chain went in, but wouldn't come out. It was hung on something. The father of one of the kids showed up and tried to free the chain, but couldn't. He hooked the chain to his pick-up truck and pulled a ten foot long, fully grown, alligator out of the drain. The kids quit "fishing" in the storm drain after that.

Somewhere I have a picture of my caiman. Polaroid had just come out with the "Swinger" camera, probably the first widely available high-speed, instant developing film camera. In the picture I am kneeling behind our Ford Fairlane holding the caiman by the head. What is funny is that the cat, a solid white cat that Josh had brought home from Auburn, named "Cat", is floating, about 24 inches above the ground, in a very rattled state.

The cat had come over to check out the caiman (it probably looked sort of like a big, rough, chameleon, or anole, to the cat). When the cat got too close the caiman switched its tail and the cat went off like a shot. At that precise instant, my brother had hit the shutter button on the "Swinger" and the cat, in the air above the caiman, was frozen for all time.

When I was older, ten or eleven, I traded a bicycle for an American Alligator. It came in a big, flimsy box that Scott and I wrestled all the way home from the previous owner's house.

This wasn't like the caiman—that was only about

18 inches long. This was a genuine, juvenile American Alligator. This alligator was at least as long as I was tall (maybe four and a half feet) and, not surprisingly, got away from me in a few days, never to be seen again. I did get to play with it some before it got away.

Playing with alligators provides an excellent example of why rolling with the punches is important. When an alligator bites, it is looking for limbs, not body mass. Body mass is hard to deal with, but limbs break off. This alligator got me by the elbow on several occasions and, when this happens, all you can do is roll with the alligator or give up the arm. I knew this from watching Johnny Weissmuller "Tarzan" movies. As long as you can keep up with the alligator you'll be O.K. except for the bite itself. Still, a bite is a whole lot easier to deal with than the stub of an arm.

Raymond L. Ditmar's "Snakes of the World"

Raymond L. Ditmar's "Snakes of the World" laid the foundation that would lead to a life, my life, devoted to the pursuit of understanding how things work, and the idea that there is nothing that you cannot learn.

Ditmar, I was told by a next-door neighbor who apparently had some form of professional association with him, was the father of modern herpetology, and had done more to advance the study of snakes than anyone else.

This book is around three inches thick and I studied its pages until much of it was memorized. I knew all of the poisonous snakes of the world by sight regardless of continent. When the soldiers in Viet Nam were taking casualties from snakebite due to a Southeast Asian snake with the same type of venom as a cobra (i.e., neurotoxin) called the Banded Krait, I knew what they were talking about.

Unfortunately, I also knew that the only long-term survivor of multiple cobra bites was a man named Bill Haas at the Miami Serpentarium who had taken small daily doses of cobra venom for years in order to build up his tolerance to the toxin. Clearly there was no time for any kind of conditioning in order to protect the soldiers.

I studied every page and I have probably never been more passionate about anything else as I was about snakes back then.

One of the main benefits I gained was that I do not fear snakes—any snakes. To this day I find even the smallest snake enchanting. I always stop and say “Hi”!

Mama—Bipolar Normal

One of the most unusual aspects of my upbringing is that I was raised by not only a manic-depressive, but by a manic-depressive who didn't know what manic-depression was, in a time when countless psychiatric conditions were only beginning to be discussed. In the past, they would have said you had a breakdown and/or you were crazy. I do not blame mother—I know better, but it is amazing to me to think of all of the people who knew her, but didn't know about the manic-depression.

This is not too hard to understand. It is one of the main problems in diagnosing the disorder. When manic-depressives are in depression they stay in and so folks don't see them when they are feeling low. Likewise, the doctors don't often see the patients when they are manic. Manic-depressives don't go to the doctor when they are feeling good. I read of a manic-depressive that was only diagnosed correctly after they ran into their doctor at a local mall while the person was manic. At that point the doctor was finally able to put two and two together and diagnose the patient correctly.

If all you have ever known is one reality, then you assume that that reality IS reality. I did not so much understand the problem as I had a sort of feeling about it. Mostly, my brother and I just wrote it off to the fact that she got up and left before we did in the morning and came back awhile after we got home from school. She worked hard and she should get tired. My brother and I were the original latchkey kids. All of the other kids that we played with had two parents, although many of them would have probably been better off to be in the situation that we were in than to be in a house with two parents, one of whom was abusive. Many did not have two parents present since the father was in Viet Nam.

In some ways being the child of an "undocumented" manic-depressive is a dream come true. When Mama was in a manic phase she had energy running out her pores. She could keep up pretty good with my brother and me. Don't get me wrong—the lows were bad for all of us. In some way, I probably saw it as fair. Really good "good times" and really bad "bad times".

Looking back on it, I can see us just rolling along through the mania and the depression. There were diversions and neighbors who acted as "neighborhood" parents who watched out for all.

Having grown up in such unusual conditions, I am surprised that we made out as well as we did. Having studied much about the subject since, I am reminded of an interview with a woman with bipolar disorder that I read in a medical textbook. This woman was asked if she could do everything over again, if she would be bipolar. She replied, much to my surprise, that she would. She went on to talk about the intensity with which she had experienced life and the intensity of the feelings that she felt and that she passed on to others. And she talked about the lows and wearing them like a heavy coat. But she said she would rather not change things because, in her opinion, the good far outweighed the bad. She said that she had lived life more intensely and felt things more intensely than any "normal" person would ever have experienced and that was worth it to her.

Based on personal experience with my mother, I cannot imagine anything that could feel so good that it could outweigh the horrible pit of hell that is clinical depression. Then again, my mother had great company—Hemingway, Handel, and all the other greats of bipolar disorder, many of whom are from the South.

Martin Army ER

The Emergency Room at Martin Army Hospital on Fort Benning is a place I knew well. I usually "stopped by" once or twice a month. I spent so much time in the emergency room that there were nurses who remembered Mama and me by name.

The Martin Army ER was a weird place. This was during the peak years of Viet Nam and a popular way to get out of going to Viet Nam was to shoot off one of your little toes or get your hand tangled up in the action of an M-1 rifle. Later M-16 actions couldn't do anything like the damage that an M-1 action could do. So there I was waiting in the ER for a tetanus shot—I got a lot of tetanus shots as a kid.

We finally got in to see the nurse and this extremely large, black nurse came over with a clipboard and asked Mama if she was Mrs. Harding who taught at Edward A. White. Mama said that she was. The nurse said that she had had one of Mama's students in for something the other day and that the child had told her that Mrs. Harding had said that "If you eat too much, you'll get too fat, and you may die of a heart attack!"

It was times like this that mother would say that she "wanted to crawl under the rug!"

Mama apologized to the woman. All I know is that the nurse didn't take it out on me when she gave me my "weekly" dose of tetanus vaccine and maybe she heeded the advice. Probably not.

Granny

Granny was a mean, old woman. I am not sure exactly where this came from, but one of her sisters, Lila, could be pretty mean as well.

Granny ended up in Parrott in the exact same way as Grampa's two brothers' wives had. They all came to Parrott as the new schoolteacher. As each new schoolteacher arrived, the brothers, Ray, Wade, and Clint (Grampa), would evaluate the candidate and decide who was going to get this one. And that is how they all got married.

Now Grampa was not just some clerk at the cotton gin; he had gone to what I believe was a one year business school. The school was located in Valdosta, or someplace like that. I have seen the diploma so I know that this is so. He was later the town Post Master and a member of the civilian enemy aircraft spotters' corps during World War II. It was how he did his part because the Army wouldn't take him because he was the only male in the family and they had a young child, my mother. In some ways, it is a shame because Grampa was incredibly accurate with any form of firearm—pistol, rifle, or shotgun. He could take a weapon that he had never seen before and take one shot to determine where the bullet was going relative to the "sight" picture, and then proceed to hit any target at will for all remaining shots. He would have been deadly as a sniper.

Grampa and his brothers were all "catches". "Daddy Ed", their father, was a prominent local businessman and farmer, and he, and his sons, all lived reasonably comfortable lives. Rural, and not rich, but certainly comfortable. Grampa was also the nephew of the founder of the town, Uncle John Parrott.

Granny ended up with Grampa. Granny was a "Hatcher" from over at Cuthbert. She was one of four sisters—Lila, Maida, Alva, and Janie Mae, my grandmother. From what I know I believe that Janie Mae and Lila both dreamed of prominence that never came, sort of. In their old age it seemed to eat at them that they had not achieved the lofty goals that they had set for themselves. Unfortunately, Lila blamed her lack of achievement on her husband, “Uncle Dave”, and Granny blamed hers on Grampa.

Granny and Grampa had one child, my Mama. Best I can tell the three of them lived a comparably comfortable life, especially during the Great Depression. During those hard times, as always, my grandparents had a very large vegetable garden, big enough to grow vegetables for the entire year. Granny had a small storage room off the back of the farmhouse that we called, oddly enough, “The Little Room”. This room was stuffed with all forms of canned vegetables, fruits, jams, jellies, and preserves.

Being the sportsman that Grampa was, there was also a steady stream of game—mainly fish and fowl. In the Great Depression, if you didn’t have to wonder where your next meal was going to come from then you really had something. There is no doubt that many of the residents of the town had an easier time of it because of Grampa’s ability and generosity.

I am not sure Granny ever fully appreciated what she had, or maybe she did appreciate her situation, but felt she deserved more, which is more likely the case. She was jealous of her own daughter and felt that her husband paid more attention to my mother than he did to her.

Josh, had spent most of his adolescent and teen years living with my grandparents. Mama had sent him to live with them to get him away from my Daddy who had a history of being really hard on him.

Later in her life, Granny, in a fit of anger and venom, once told my mother that Josh was her child, and not my mother's. That's a pretty mean thing to say to your daughter. It was even more hurtful when you take into account that my mother took the Bible and the "Honor thy father and mother" part literally. There really was nothing mean enough that Granny could do that would cause my mother to forsake her beliefs. I have little doubt that my mother actually went so far as to question whether or not Granny's claim could actually be the case.

I have Granny's cookbook. When she died it passed to Josh, and when he died, I ended up with it. It is a thick, bookkeeping ledger and many of the recipes have been cut out of magazines or newspapers and pasted to the pages. It is a treasure trove of weirdness.

There are numerous recipes where Granny had documented "Mrs. So and So's Recipe for Whatever". Many of these recipes are footnoted with

Granny's comments about "Mrs. So and So", such as "Mrs. So and So uses ingredient, or seasoning, 'X', but I don't agree with her and I use ingredient, or seasoning, 'Y'". Or "Mrs. So and So does it this way, but that is not the Christian way. I personally always use the Christian way." She was so compulsive that the cookbook has recipes that are repeated for different portion sizes such as "Biscuits for Four" followed immediately by "Biscuits for Eight" and so on. The same for pots of coffee divided by the number of cups per pot. She even went so far as to try and second guess how much each person would eat based on experience and current situation and when the preacher came for Sunday dinner once or twice a year there was usually just enough for everyone to get what she felt was the correct amount of each dish. Most of the time there were no leftovers in her refrigerator, but then again she had come from a time when they didn't have refrigerators or a lot of food.

One year, in the sixties, Granny got wall-to-wall carpet for the living room and foyer. Wall-to-wall carpet was new at the time. I am not sure that Granny was not colorblind because she picked this ugly, brownish colored carpet. Then again Georgia is covered with red clay and she may have been thinking ahead, but that really wasn't her style. At the same time she had all of the fireplaces in the house bricked up and replaced by more fashionable (in her mind) gas heaters. This robbed us all of a favorite treat in the fall when the sugar cane harvest happened. We would sit in front of the fireplace in the living room and peel the sugar cane, cut it into bite size pieces, and crush the juice out with our teeth. Then we would throw what was left of the cane into the fire, which provided a hissing and popping treat as the crushed, wet, cane hit the hot coals (literally) of the fire. We burned coal, not wood, and so the fireplaces were about as neat as you could have since coal burns almost completely, and with significantly less smoke than with a wood fire.

One day after my brothers and I had been messing around outdoors, we came into the living room, which was also Granny and Grampa's bedroom, that was strategically located so that there was no way for anyone to get to the kitchen at night without going through that room unless you went around the outside of the house.

Keep in mind that Josh could do no wrong in Granny's eyes and, in her mind, his "perfect" behavior was the result of her efforts and her efforts alone.

Nate and I were playing on the floor and Granny came into the room. "Get up off the floor! You're going to get the carpet dirty!" she said.

Josh asked her "How are they going to get the floor any dirtier than walking on it? Their shoes are dirtier than their britches!"

In a rare exhibit of logic, Granny was forced to accept his reasoning and we got to play on the floor—after we took our shoes off.

Mama said Granny used to spank her with a hairbrush when she was a child and Granny would tell her to stop crying as she paddled her. Somehow, it was reasonable to Granny that you could spank a child into stopping crying.

I don't really understand why my Aunt Birdee later decided to try to blow up Granny, but given Granny's meanness it was apparently a moment of clarity on Aunt Birdee's part.

Storeowner Defends Self—Robber Killed

Grampa killed a man during the Great Depression.

Grampa had a small store in downtown Parrott. A man, who had obviously seen better times in the past, came into Grampa's store one evening just as he was getting ready to close up for the night.

The man was obviously distressed. He grabbed a loaf of bread and headed for the door. Grampa retrieved a small .38 caliber Smith & Wesson handgun from the cigar box under the counter where he kept it and yelled at the man to stop.

The man stopped, turned, and fired one shot at Grampa, hitting him in the thumb of the hand he was holding the gun in, knocking his thumbnail completely off. Grampa held on to the gun, fired once, and killed the man instantly.

It was very sad, because from what I know of Grampa he would have given the bread to the man if he had asked for it.

He would not talk about the incident; in fact, I do not recall him ever talking about it. The story I know was told to me by Mama and Josh. I have no reason to doubt the truthfulness of the story. One thing's for sure and that is that if Grampa ever fired at you, he would hit you, unless he intended not to.

Aunt Birdee

Lewis Grizzard was a sort of modern day, Southern Mark Twain who wrote for the Atlanta Journal Constitution, or some big newspaper in Atlanta. Grizzard once said something to the effect that "The South is not like the North. In the North they hide their crazy people away, but in the South we bring them out and parade them around!" No one ever hid Aunt Birdee; she wouldn't have it and she did the parading around all own her own—no assistance required.

Birdee has a strong, and odd, belief in God that is in some ways similar to Mama's mix of evangelism, superstition, and folklore. She believes that King Juan Carlos is the Anti-Christ because she has a paperback book that says that he is. I have heard many guesses as to who the Anti-Christ is, if he is, in fact, among us—Osama Bin Laden, Muktada Al-Sadir, etc., but I have never heard of Juan Carlos being on the list.

Aunt Birdee once told me a story about some "English boys", as she called them, who had come to Dawson, or Albany, for their flight training during World War II. According to Aunt Birdee, there were two young aviators and Mama was paired up with one of the aviators and Aunt Birdee with the other.

On one of their days off the two young aviators had apparently commandeered one of their training aircraft and flown over to Parrott for a little "spoonin'". While they were there, Aunt Birdee's beau offered to take her for a ride.

According to Aunt Birdee, the plane took off and then crashed shortly after take-off. Both occupants survived. The training aircraft of the day were pretty sturdily built if for no other reason than lightweight materials didn't exist at the time. They did not go very fast either and they also usually generated a lot of lift which allowed them to fly at very slow speeds making landings smoother which was important since there usually wasn't a runway to land on, just some grass or dirt. Aunt Birdee was shaken, but soon got over the incident.

The boys apparently stayed over and the following day they repaired the airplane after parts were flown in by another training aircraft of the same type. They prepared to return to their postings. Aunt Birdee's beau offered to give her another ride in the airplane that had brought the parts. Now, nobody ever claimed that Aunt Birdee was the cautious type, and she agreed to try it again.

Again, according to Aunt Birdee, the "new" airplane took off and it, also, crashed shortly after take-off. Aunt Birdee was more descriptive when she talked about the second crash, no doubt because, having previously been involved in an airplane crash, in the same type of airplane, she was better prepared for what was happening.

Once again, both occupants walked away from the crash. To my knowledge Aunt Birdee never got into an airplane ever again.

Aunt Birdee was a wild child. She left Parrott and went to New York to pursue the Bohemian life around the time Mama went off to the University of Georgia.

Birdee eventually won the heart of a young man in New York City who managed entertainers. He later went on to manage some popular, big-name singer during the 70's.

He was sane and the marriage lasted only long enough for my two cousins to be born. Both were stunningly beautiful young women. The youngest went on to be crowned a beauty queen.

After he and Aunt Birdee parted ways, Aunt Birdee returned to the family home in Parrott. The children were divided up between the two parents and Kristen ended up living with her father, and Jeanie ended up living with Aunt Birdee.

At one point, Aunt Birdee decided that there might be a way for her to combine her fondness for cheap, sweet wine and her love of art. Aunt Birdee had fancied herself an artist for years even though she lacked much talent or formal training. When she went to New York her plan had been to room with her cousin Merle. Merle really was an artist and a very talented one. She was also stunningly beautiful. I have seen a painting of her and she looks sort of like the nymphs that Maxfield Parrish painted.

Unfortunately, Merle had gotten involved with a married businessman who apparently had promised to leave his wife and marry Merle. Merle died when she fell, some say jumped, beneath a subway train after being jilted by the man.

Josh told me the story. According to him after Merle died, Grampa, who was very fond of his niece, had hired the Pinkertons to track down the truth. Supposedly they had reported back that her death was most likely a suicide, but the official story remained that her death was an accident in order to spare the family, and Merle, any shame.

So, Aunt Birdee began to paint simple floral designs on old wine bottles. She called them "My aaaahhhtttt" (art). I don't believe she ever sold any of the decorated bottles but I did once find a few underneath my grandparents' house. Apparently, Aunt Birdee had given Granny a few of her creations at some point and Granny had promptly banished them to under the house with the potato and onion racks.

In many ways, Aunt Birdee was the worst person that Mama could have been around. Aunt Birdee shared Mama's odd form of Christianity. The idea of God coming down and dabbling directly in peoples' lives was very real to both of them. Several times in the past, Aunt Birdee was probably directly responsible for Mama's depression after she stopped taking her meds based on Aunt Birdee's chiding that if she had enough faith she wouldn't need the meds. So Mama would gather her faith, stop taking her meds, and, then later, come crashing down into a depressive phase.

The last time I saw Aunt Birdee in all her splendor was after my mother's funeral. We had all gone over to see Aunt Birdee's house—my brother, his wife and kids, my girlfriend, Nina, and me. We took a camera and as soon as Aunt Birdee saw the camera, she began to pose on the front porch of the beautiful Victorian Gingerbread house in which she lived. She was the complete “ham”. I told her that she was a “Hoot” and she spent much of the next hour making sure that everyone knew that she was a “Hoot”. It was like the gamekeeper in “Twelfth Night” that after being called “an ass” makes it a point to tell all his friends that he is “an ass”, all the while thinking that this is somehow a compliment. My cousin Jeanie laughed. I do not think Aunt Birdee really understood what a “Hoot” was since this is more of a Western term than a Southern one. In Georgian the synonym is probably “Nut”.

THE MONKEY BARN

My cousin Jeanie has had a tough life. Saddled with caring for her mother, Aunt Birdee, from a young age, Jeanie is one strong woman. She has been through the mill and I think the world of her.

When Jeanie was staying with friends in Dawson while Aunt Birdee was off under observation after the dynamite incident, Granny started a vicious rumor that Jeanie must have been prostituting herself in Dawson to pay for her room and board since she had no other visible form of income and surely these people wouldn't take her in for free! Apparently, Granny could not believe that non-family folks could be so generous unless there was a catch. That is just an example of how Granny thought about things.

There was never one iota of truth to the rumor. I have never understood why Granny would do something like this to such a sweet, innocent young woman. Granny was just plain mean.

At some point Jeanie moved to Sasser to try and gain some distance, privacy, and find a job. It was close enough that she could get to Aunt Birdee's within a half hour if needed, but far enough away so that her privacy would not be intruded upon. While she was living in Sasser, Jeanie became involved with a local businessman who owned a bar called "The Monkey Barn".

The guy's wife knew about Jeanie, but, as is common in many Southern marriages, divorce was out of the question. Appearance is many times much more important than truth or happiness in that culture. So Jeanie became the manager of "The Monkey Barn" and the relationship continued for many years.

When you walked in to "The Monkey Barn" you saw the reason for the name. The front wall, on either side of the front door, formed a glassed in enclosure approximately two feet deep and running from floor to ceiling. In the enclosure were ten, or so, small monkeys similar in appearance to spider monkeys. The monkeys could pass over the top of the door way so that they could get to either of the large enclosures.

At one point during Jeanie's tenure as manager, concerned citizens tried to get the monkeys removed from the "inhumane" environment and treatment. I guess the local self-righteous figured that the music played in the bar was somehow demoralizing, or demeaning, to the monkeys. Jeanie fought the removal.

Zoologists from the University of Georgia and several zoos descended upon "The Monkey Barn" to conduct an assessment of conditions.

Now, this particular type of monkey does not normally do well in captivity and reproduction in captivity by this species is unheard of, but the monkeys at "The Monkey Barn" were thriving and one monkey even gave birth while the scientists were there conducting their assessment.

In the end, the scientists determined that not only was the environment humane but they intended to take what they had seen back to their respective collections and attempt to reproduce the success that they had observed at the bar.

Score one for the monkeys, zero for the self-righteous "concerned" citizens.

The monkeys were finally sent to the zoos after the owner was suddenly killed in a car accident one rainy night. Unfortunately, for Jeanie, he apparently assumed that he would always be around to take care of her and so he had not made any preparation for his inevitable demise.

I'm told the guy's wife immediately shut down "The Monkey Barn". Apparently, the hate she felt for Jeanie outweighed her greed, since it would have been much more to her financial advantage if "The Monkey Barn" had remained open.

People in the South can be funny like that.

“Dreckly”

Grampa had a single standard reply that he used to answer almost every question—“Dreckly”.

I grew up hearing this unusual and versatile word. When I first considered this word I was just old enough that I wasn’t going to let on that I didn’t know what it meant and learned to use the word fairly proficiently without even knowing what it meant. Mama’s training of us with phonics meant that we could do a pretty good job of spelling the word even if we could not recall ever seeing it written. It seemed to be a “spoken only” sort of word. That was O.K. because I knew there were other words that people used, but that you didn’t see written. Words like “ain’t”, which is part of any true Southerner’s vocabulary, but which we were taught was not a word in school, even though it had a spelling, and was regularly used. So I just figured that “Dreckly” was one of those unwritten words.

The problem was that while I could sort of see “ain’t” as a contraction of “isn’t not”, a more emphatic form of “isn’t”, I had no clue where “Dreckly” came from.

I never questioned the word until I was nine or ten when my curiosity got the better of me and I asked Mama what the deal was.

“Directly!” Where did they get that? “Directly” had to do with directions like “Go Directly To Jail. Do Not Pass Go. Do Not Collect $200”, like in the game Monopoly. Not a general reply! This “Directly” had to do with time!

Not to Grampa. To him it was a versatile word that could be used to calm any situation with the promise that all would be taken care of.

Question: “When are we going?”

Reply: “Dreckly”.

Question: “Can I shoot the shotgun?

Reply: “Dreckly”.

Question: “Think we’ll catch any fish?”

Reply: “Dreckly”.

Grampa had gotten his family through the Great Depression. He had learned to economize in all he did...including his words.

He had other words like that. I was ten before I figured out that “cottages” was not a word that could be used interchangeably for both small houses and bullets. Grampa's pronunciation of "cartridges" was "cottages".

Harmony Church

When I was around eleven, Viet Nam was really booming! Cronkite brought us the body count every evening. Having grown up making use of the swimming pools that were available on Fort Benning, we were always on the lookout for a less crowded pool. On Main Post, at the Officer's Club, it was wall-to-wall elbows. The pool at Sand Hill, nearer to our house, was, sort of, the minority swimming pool and mother didn't think it was safe. Not for fear of the blacks or Hispanics (remember, we're all equal), but because most of the kids that hung out at Sand Hill were a lot bigger than we were and she was afraid that they would pick on us.

Around the same time, Mama had learned of a small church, way out off Main Post where there were young men who were scared about where they were going and what they were facing. These young men were trying to make their peace with God before they got to meet him in person, which would happen soon enough for many of them. Never was there a place more made for my Mama!

Mama started hauling us out to Harmony Church on Sunday evenings instead of going to the evening service at our church which we could usually get out of since she would not be too far away should we set fire to the neighborhood or some such thing. The young men we met there were inspirational. Three to five soldiers would get together and form a singing group. There were several of these groups and they would each, in turn, sing a song as part of the service, and they were really, really, good.

Most of these young men were black, though not all, and here is my mother taking her children to this far off church and letting us play with these guys and then, God forbid!, inviting the whole lot over to our house after the service for fried chicken, green beans, biscuits, and mashed potatoes and gravy for all. What would the neighbors think?! Obviously Mama wasn't in depression when she would do this. She also didn't pay much attention to the neighbors when she was doing something that the Bible said you should do.

I have often wondered how many of those young

me made it back. Hopefully, all of them did. Probably not.

Anyway, the high point of our association with Harmony Church and those out there was when we learned that there was a Harmony Church Swimming Pool. An Olympic-size swimming pool with high and low diving boards that never had more than five people in it at any time. There was also a large, rarely used, gymnasium adjacent to the pool where you could change and shower.

The gym is where they would lay out large wrestling mats and then line up the soldiers with only their boxers and T-shirt's on, and at the end of the line were a couple of doctors with this huge, Medusa-like, injection device that probably gave the recruits all injections needed before heading to Viet Nam in a single shot.

Oh yeah! The mats. It was funny because we would sit up in the bleachers while waiting for Mama to come pick us up and watch as just about one out of three passed out and hit the mats after receiving their injections.

Click, Click, Boom! and another one would hit the mats! It didn't take much to amuse us at times.

Insanity. Just Plain Insanity.

During one of the big troop build-ups in the sixties, the Army had these firing ranges that had "active" targets. The targets had human silhouettes painted on them and were mounted on spring-loaded bases. The targets could be popped up as the soldiers advanced across the firing range and the soldiers were supposed to engage the targets when they popped up.

During this time there was some lieutenant, or captain, who did not believe that the soldiers were reacting appropriately—they weren't scared of the targets. This is still a problem today—getting someone to react with adrenalin in a simulation environment. So, to add some realism, this officer had the targets outfitted with .22 caliber rifles with "live" ammunition. Now, when the targets popped up, they fired. "Live" rounds!

This officer was finally removed after the second,

or third, soldier was killed by one of the "active" targets.

Driving Mules with Bully

When I was around six, or seven, we still had the mule barn on the farm and it was still functional, complete with a pair of mules. Mules are unusual animals. Anyone who has spent time around them will tell you that there are good mules and bad mules, no in between. If they are bad, they are bad, and if they are good, they are good.

Bully was a black farmhand and Grampa's right-hand man on the farm during much of my childhood. Bully taught me how to drive a mule team. Bully was also the source of all the superior pork barbeque on the farm. As they said, "He didn't throw away anything but the squeal."

Bully was a sort of like Uncle Remus to me—full of advice and counsel that sounded great to me, but I don't know if Grampa would have agreed with all of it. But remember, Mama taught us that everybody was the same. She took her Bible literally—if not superstitiously.

Bully taught me how to get the mules out, harness them, drive them to town, bring them home, and put them away. At my height, it was like working with elephants. Mules are generally large anyway, but they are huge when you are six. Bully taught me the calls "Gee" and "Haw" to get the mules to turn to the right or to the left. He let me drive the team as long as he was with me. Too cool!

Bully remained on the farm until he finally went to live with his daughter and son-in-law in the last few years of his life. He lived in a house down in the "Quarters" that he rented from Grampa, and then Granny, for most of his adult life. Josh, and later myself, let him stay for free as soon as Granny was out of the picture after she went to the Nursing Home.

I went by to see Bully every time I went back to the farm. Late in his life, I asked him what he wanted if I could get him anything. He said that he would really like a pig to raise. I asked him how much he needed to get a good pig. He said $25 would get a good, young pig. He would usually raise the pig for a year and then slaughter the pig in the fall. I gave Bully $25 each year for a new pig until he finally went to live with his daughter. Bully only lasted a couple of years after he left the farm. In some ways, the farm may have kept him going. I can't imagine what it would be like to have lived in the same, small place for almost your entire life and then move, for the first time, when you were in your seventies.

Red-Winged Blackbird Dinner

Grampa had one hard and fast rule regarding hunting to which he held us and that rule was that if you're going to kill it, you damn well better be prepared to eat it. He would cut you some slack with fish. You're not looking at the fish when you hook it so there is less control in that situation.

One day Grampa and I were fishing by ourselves. Grampa had brought the .410 shotgun in the boat, in case a water moccasin, or rattlesnake, should threaten the outing. It was not unusual to have a water moccasin try to catch a rest from swimming by climbing into the boat with you.

I saw a red-winged blackbird in the cattails and told Grampa that I was going to shoot it. He said very quietly "If you shoot it, you're going to eat it!" I fired. The bird fell and then Grampa started paddling the boat forward into the cattails, so that I could retrieve the bird. I did. And I also got to clean it, and have it for dinner after he had Granny cook it for me. Everybody else got bass. Everybody but me.

Red-winged blackbird is not very good eating and I have never harmed a red-winged blackbird since.

When I was in my twenties I once shot a coot at a significant range so that I could not really tell that it was not a duck. When I paddled the canoe out to retrieve my "duck" I found that it was instead a coot. In keeping with Grampa's training I cleaned it, cooked it, and ate it. Coot is right in there with red-winged blackbird on the culinary scale. All I knew was that "If you shoot it, you eat it!"

Armed Forces Day Downtown

When I was ten, Sgt. Little, my downhill side, next-door neighbor, came back from Viet Nam. I had only had any experience with his wife, and she was pretty mean, in my opinion. Sgt. Little was a mechanic in the Army on Fort Benning. This was roughly my second year of studying all things mechanical and it seemed to me that Sgt. Little clearly had the neatest job in the Army. My Daddy commanded a truck company, but Sgt. Little got to take them apart.

Sgt. Little, as it turned out, was actually a pretty neat guy. Several times he took me with him to the motor pool on Fort Benning when he would have to do some small thing on a Saturday. He was the first person to let me steer a car. He had a Volkswagen Beetle and it was probably the first, or second, foreign car I ever rode in. On the way to the motor pool he pulled out a cigarette and some matches and said "Hold the wheel." "Whoa!" I thought to myself. "Hold the wheel!" he said. I took hold of the wheel and all of a sudden it was "Wow! I'm driving!" He lit his cigarette, took back the wheel, and then told me that lighting a cigarette while driving was a good way to get into an accident. To him it wasn't the smoking that was dangerous, it was lighting the cigarette that could get you killed. There's that funny Southern way of thinking about things again.

U.S. Army tanks of the day had white enamel interiors and very few of the switches and levers were labeled. Apparently, this was an effort to limit the enemy's ability to use our own assets against us. Not to worry though, Sgt. Little told me what the switches and levers were and how they worked and, in the process, showed me how to start one of the behemoths. Too Cool!

Columbus was a classic "up and coming" city of the day. Broadway, downtown, is a divided street with a broad, manicured green strip with fountains and concrete benches between the two roadways which were one-way in either direction. Fort Benning was an important part of Columbus. Columbus' economy depended on Fort Benning.

Each year on Armed Forces Day, Columbus would invite the Army to show off their stuff on Broadway. The Army would bring an incredible assortment of military vehicles and systems and set them up all up and down Broadway on the green strip.

On Armed Forces Day, the year that Sgt. Little showed me how to start the tank, Mama took us downtown to see the displays.

After some reconnaissance, I located a tank I was familiar with on display, made my way up the hull, and then down into the turret. There was a private, or corporal, or sergeant (I don't remember which) inside "minding the store". I made my way to the driver's station and then asked the attending soldier if I could start it up? He replied "Sure, if you think you can!" Little did he know...

The tank sprang almost instantly to life. These were diesel powered vehicles and not the slow starting, turbine powered, main battle tanks that we have today. With the starting of the tank came the huge belch of black smoke and the accompanying rumble of the large diesel engine.

I thought that the soldier was going to have a heart attack or bang his head at the very least, he had moved so quickly. He pulled the fuel kill and the beast went back to sleep. Before much could be said, the soldier's commanding officer, a lieutenant I think, showed up wanting to know why he had started the tank up with all of the people around? I didn't hang around, but I am pretty sure that the officer reminded his subordinate about the incident for some time afterward on a regular basis. I can almost hear it, the commander telling his subordinate "So a ten year old kid climbs in here and just starts up the tank? Yeah, right!"

A few years later, we would attend the Armed Forces Day celebration, which had since been moved to a parade ground on Fort Benning at that point, and witness one of the earliest public demonstrations of a new military capability—rappelling into battle from a helicopter hovering above the battlefield.

Unfortunately, it was also a deadly demonstration. During the rappelling demonstration, one soldier became entangled in his gear and was killed. The helicopter exited the reviewing area with the dead soldier suspended about midway between the helicopter and the ground, although it was not known that the soldier was already dead at that point.

Pulling the Snake, the Bush, and the Line

Summer evenings in Georgia can seem to have endless twilight times, especially if you are somewhere where there aren't a lot of city lights to block the view of the stars. There is also not a lot to do in the dark when you are a kid. We didn't spend endless hours glued to the television back then. In fact, my mother never even had a color television until after I graduated from high school. This forces you to be creative. Consequently, we spent most of our time outside. A lot of it in the dark.

We didn't have much money, either. A $5 bill is the most money I had ever had at one time until I started working when I was twelve. We had to be creative, and, ideally, whatever we came up with needed to be durable.

Now, most folks in the South don't like snakes. In

fact, most folks are afraid of them, regardless of the type of snake. This is probably related to the prevalent Biblical focus the locals have. Consequently, most Southerners will never let a snake escape unscathed if they can help it. It is this weakness that we preyed upon.

What you do is you take an old, preferably dark, nylon stocking (this is before panty hose) and loosely fill it with rags to form the body of the "snake". Tie the head off with a length of fishing line (10# monofilament fishing line is difficult to see at a distance especially at night) and attach a length of line 15' to 20' in length to "pull the snake" with. Next, find an appropriately slow part of a road, preferably a dirt road, as the "snake" will last longer if it isn't a hard surfaced road. A hard surface road works fine in a pinch.

Place the "snake" on one side of the road. Run the line to the other side of the road and take up a covert position on that side. Then you wait. When the headlights of an approaching car illuminate the "snake", give a firm, but short tug on the line so that the "snake" moves across the road toward you, the "operator".

In most cases, the driver will see the "snake" and slam on the brakes in order to go back and check that the job is complete and the “snake” is dead, or at least not moving anymore. Usually the car will back up over the snake far enough so that the snake’s mortality can be assessed. At this point, wait until the headlights of the backing car illuminate the “snake” and then give another tug on the line so that the “snake” continues to move across the road toward the “operator”.

If you’re good at presenting a reasonably lifelike “snake”, you can keep the driver going back and forth over the “snake” until you finally get it all the way across the road.

A variation on the “snake” is “Pulling the Bush”. “Pulling the Bush” works similarly, but is more of a one-time thing because it’s fairly obvious that a bush can’t move by itself. You should be prepared to run after “Pulling the Bush”.

First, you need to find a small, bushy plant and trim off anything that isn’t bush. Attach a piece of monofilament to the bush. Depending on the size of the bush you may need 20#, or heavier, line. Run the line to the other side of the road to your covert location, take cover, and wait.

As with the “snake”, wait until the headlights of the approaching car illuminate the “bush” and, when it is lined up just ahead of the front of the car, you yank the line, pulling the bush into the oncoming car's path. Watch the brake lights. Listen to the squeal of the tires. Then RUN!

I am serious about the "RUN" part. A snake is one thing, but after the bush jumps out in front of the car, the people will stop and they may very well get out and come after you. I gave up pulling the bush after we "Pulled the Bush" on a Police car and narrowly escaped. It is important that you know the area well and have an escape plan when "Pulling the Bush".

The final variation on this theme is by far the simplest and, in some ways, the most spectacular. It is called "Pulling the Line".

The only thing required for "Pulling the Line" is the monofilament fishing line. You should use 10#, or 20#, line.

"Pulling the Line" involves using the unsuspecting car to "pull the line". Start by determining the approximate height of the car's windshield. Locate two trees, one on either side of the road, and string the fishing line between the two trees such that it is at a height approximately level with the middle of the windshield.

When a car approaches, pull the string taut and tie it off. You do not want to be holding the line when the car hits. Provided there is some lip to the window frame, the line will be caught by the window frame and pulled until the breaking point. As the line is pulled taut, it sounds sort of like a nylon guitar string being wound up very tight and very fast until it finally snaps. The heavier the line, the louder the report, when the line finally snaps. It sounds really strange inside the car, especially if the windows are rolled up.

Obviously, "Pulling the Line" only works once for each set up, but the reward is sometimes greater. When you don't have TV, and computers, and video games, you have to be creative.

Phone Pranks

I, along with many young men from my time, made use of the phone as a source of near endless entertainment. Endless in the sense that you could do the prank once, which was the funniest part of all, and then tell the story of the prank over and over again to retrieve even more humor from the action. Caller-ID hadn't been invented, and so the chance of getting caught when making a prank phone call was slim to none. Phone pranks were so prevalent that I even ran across a few sharp storeowners who had unusual comebacks to the "classics". Like when Mr. Arnold, who owned the pharmacy at the nearby shopping center (what we would call a strip mall today), was asked if he had Prince Albert in a can (a common brand of pipe tobacco and probably what Steve Douglas smoked on the "My Three Sons" TV show). He replied "No, he got out yesterday and I haven't been able to catch him yet!" Mr. Arnold was pretty sharp. He was supposed to say, "yes," and the prankster would say, "Well let him out. He's suffocating!"

Here are some of the best ones.

Ring, ring, ring.

Prankster: This is the phone company and we are working on the phone line down the street and we seem to have a lot of slack in the line and we were wondering if you could help us out?

Called: Sure. What do you need?

Prankster: Could you grab your phone line and give a good tug?

What follows is the sound of the dial tone after the line is broken.

Ring, ring, ring.

Prankster (calling the grocery store): Yes, do you have pickled pig's feet?

Called: Yes, we do!

Prankster: Well stand behind the counter and no one will notice!

Ring, ring, ring.

Prankster (calling a filling station, usually full-service back then): Hello. Could you tell me what you're getting a gallon for premium?

Called: 18 cents a gallon.

Prankster: What do you get for a quart of 30 weight (oil)?

Called: 15 cents a quart.

Prankster: Do you sell prophylactics?

Called: Yes.

Prankster: Let me hear you blow one up!

Like I said, we didn't have color TV, or computers, or video games, or money, for that matter. Necessity *is* the mother of invention.

Grampa and the "Flip"

I have a "treasure trunk" that belonged to Josh. In the box, which is actually an old (early 1900's) carpenter's tool chest, are almost all of the remaining toys that Grampa carved for Mama and the grandchildren. There is a small canoe with seats and paddles that he carved out of aromatic cedar from a tree that still stands in the yard by the garage on the farm. There is the last remaining puzzle that Grampa carved. It is an interlocking piece puzzle and Grampa probably carved five or six for me during my childhood. Only one of the ones that Josh had is left. He carved them in different sizes and they were sort of a forerunner of the "Rubic's Cube".

There is also a "flip", or what most would call a slingshot. Grampa carved it for Josh when he was around 10 years old. Grampa fitted it with a sling of string, leather, and heavy rubber bands and gave it to him.

Grampa was working downtown Parrott running the cotton gin and warehouse for Mr. Dunwoody when he gave the “Flip” to Josh. Josh took the “Flip” and went off to wage war on the local flora and fauna with his new weapon.

A short time later, Josh returned, handed the “Flip” to Grampa, and said “This flip is no good! You can’t hit anything with this thing!”

Grampa took the “Flip” without a word and picked up a small stone off of the ground. He placed the stone in the pocket of the sling and said “See that sparrow over there across the way?” Josh said “Yes.” Grampa said “I am going to skip this stone in front of the sparrow and it is going to bounce off the ground and hit the sparrow in the head.” Josh watched. Grampa took aim and let the stone fly. Just as he had said, the stone hit the ground, bounced once, and hit the sparrow in the head killing it. He handed the “Flip” to Josh and said “Seems like it works to me”.

Grampa wouldn’t tell you that you were wrong. He would calmly show you.

Mr. Dunwoody and Terry

Mr. Dunwoody was one of the richest, if not the richest, men in Terrell County. He was definitely the richest man in Parrott. Mr. Dunwoody was a strange sort of guy. He was a large, rotund man. He owned the cotton gin and the only cotton warehouse in Parrott. He was essentially the "Bank" in Parrott after the real bank closed. He imported palm trees and lined the main street of downtown Parrott. The palm trees had to be temporarily removed when a western movie was filmed in downtown Parrott in the 70's (they were replaced after the filming was complete). He built a Spanish hacienda-style house with stucco walls, a red tile roof, and marble floors for his wife, the love of his life (besides money), and never went back into the house after his wife died there. Mama said that Grampa told her that Mr. Dunwoody kept the housekeeper on for years after his wife's death, having her keep the house clean, like she had left it, as if waiting for his wife's return. The house is still there and, to my knowledge, no one has ever lived there since. It would not surprise me if Mr. Dunwoody left some kind of stipulation in his will that the house was not to ever be occupied again. It is easily the most splendid house in Parrott, although it was showing signs of deterioration the last time I saw it. On the Parrott-scale, it is truly a fine work of Mexican hacienda-style architecture with the requisite terra-cotta roof—probably the only terra-cotta roof in a fifty-mile radius, at least at the time that it was built. I believe it was built in the 1940's or 1950's.

Josh married his high school sweetheart shortly after he graduated from Auburn. Her name was Terry Caldwell, of the Albany Caldwells. She was thin and blond and looked like an escapee from a "Beach Blanket Bingo"-type surfer movie to me. He was smitten. They moved to Dallas. Shortly after, around six weeks or so, she returned to Georgia complaining that the Texas climate aggravated her allergies *and* that she wasn't sure if she loved him. They divorced shortly afterward, and as far as I know, she is still in Albany, or maybe Dawson. Actually, she would more likely be in Atlanta. I think she had visions of grandeur.

Much later, when I was older, he told me the whole story, which he hadn't known until afterward. After hearing the story I had to agree that it was better that he was no longer with her. As it turns out, Mr. Dunwoody, whom Grampa had worked for most of his adult life, had an affair with, the now Mrs. Caldwell and she had become pregnant with Terry. Terry's mother was unmarried at the time. Mr. Dunwoody wasn't.

Mr. Caldwell worked for Mr. Dunwoody, and, after assessing the situation, Mr. Dunwoody convinced Mr. Caldwell to marry Terry's mother and convinced Terry's mother to marry Mr. Caldwell. Supposedly, he provided the couple with a stipend to pay for anything that Terry needed. Terry's mother had to marry Mr. Caldwell, or somebody, or be labeled as a "woman of the town". Terry's mother, like Terry, could apparently identify a deal when she saw one and Mr. Caldwell and she were married. When Josh learned the whole story, I think he may have felt lucky to have dodged the "money pit" that Terry was. Given the subordinate position that Grampa held relative to Mr. Dunwoody, I believe Josh felt lucky to have escaped involvement in the tangled mess, but it still hurt him and ended up being the first of his three failed marriages. Josh truly loved her.

Josh

Josh was born Joshua Swint, son of Brandon and Mattie Swint. Brandon took off sometime after they were married. It was probably somewhere around, what was probably, my mother's third or fourth depressive phase of her bipolar cycling since they had been married. He later killed himself after he developed an inoperable brain tumor. He killed himself at almost the exact same age as his son killed himself.

Josh was small as a child. Frank Lloyd Wright's parents gave him blocks to play with. Grampa gave Josh two small cans of paint. Josh was bright and gifted artistically. Later in his life, he was asked by the Industrial Design Department at Auburn University, his alma mater, to come back to Auburn to teach, even though he held no advanced degree or teaching credentials. What he did have was a portfolio of successful design projects. He designed the body and the interior of the original Air Trans people mover at Dallas-Fort Worth International Airport while he was working for Ling-Temco-Vought (LTV) after he graduated from Auburn. Josh had ended up at LTV as part of avoiding service in Viet Nam. He got out of it first because of an educational deferment because he was enrolled in a program that could conceivably aid the "police action" in Viet Nam and, then, because he went to work in the aerospace industry after he graduated.

He stayed at LTV just long enough to avoid the war. Like Grampa, Josh was an excellent shot with any firearm. He, like Grampa, would have been deadly in battle. After LTV, he and a group of other engineers and designers that he had known at LTV formed a small design firm named Visual Identities (VI). He worked for VI for another few years before taking his final position working for someone else at Creative Enterprises.

Toward the end of his life, he operated Harding Design and Fabrication making "fake" antique signage and architectural graphics for the Bennigan's and Steak & Ale restaurant chains. I worked for him for a time and took over the business, and operated it for a couple of years, after his death. If you have ever been in a Bennigan's restaurant, you have probably seen his designs and our work.

He was truly amazing as an artist. I can remember as a child watching him draw whatever we had asked him to draw, and giggling uncontrollably as we watched the images emerge, perfect in every way—perspective, lighting, composition, and execution.

I remember one time, late at night, at the Chicken House Sign Shop—the shop was in an old chicken house where he had added a concrete floor. I was trying to paint the water line on some toy sailboat that we were making for Bennigan's and I wasn't having much luck even though we had made a tool to help lay out the line.

Josh was pretty buzzed from his poison of choice, Coors Light. He came into the shop and asked what I was doing. I told him and he kind of chuckled. He took the brush, and even though he was pretty well toasted, he made one stroke and painted the water line as perfectly as if it had been painted by a million dollar robotic system. He handed the brush back to me and, much like when Grampa had handed him back the "flip", said, "So?"

During the spring that he would have been forty years old, I was back in school although I had not yet settled on Mathematics as a major. I was working for Josh part time and also part time, running statistical analyses, for Dr. Adams from the Nursing Department and Dr. Peterson from the Economics Department at the University of Texas. I had not been out to the shop for a couple of days and I decided to go by and see what was up.

When I got to Josh's place, Cracker and Jack (his Brittany Spaniel and Black Labrador, both working hunting dogs) were both inside the fence and they were also both obviously upset about something.

I went to the chicken house and the light was on, but Josh wasn't there. I walked to the guesthouse, where we cleaned all the paintbrushes, but he wasn't there, either.

I finally went to the house and made a pass through, but still didn't find him.

The smell was strange. It was something that I had never smelled before. Not overpowering, but definitely strong and foreign.

I finally made a pass through his bedroom and into the bathroom that was accessible from both his bedroom and the hall and it was there that I found him slumped in the bathtub, wearing a clean shirt and jeans as if he had gotten ready to go out. There was only one thing wrong—he had a very large hole in his left forehead.

When you get shot from point blank range the projectile is the least of your worries. The thing that you have to worry about is the expanding gas from the powder charge. Josh's head looked like someone had stuck a high-pressure hose into his left forehead and squeezed the handle. He had the presence of mind to get in to the bathtub so that the tile would deflect the bullet and, most likely, keep it in the room. He would not have wanted to hurt anyone else accidentally. Also, the mess would be contained in the tub and be easier to clean up. It sounds strange, I know, but I am almost sure that was his rationale for getting into the tub to end it all.

I took the weapon away from him; a .357 Magnum Smith & Wesson Model 19 Combat Magnum, and laid it on the floor outside of the tub. There was a small piece of his skull lying on the floor next to where I had laid the gun down.

I cried.

After a few minutes I went to the phone and called the Police. This is before 911. His suicide was by far the biggest Police event they had had in recent years, if not ever.

The cops finally arrived, but not before

overshooting the driveway several times and having to turn around and come back on the narrow two lane road. They finally made it into the driveway and ushered me outside the house. About 30 minutes passed before the investigating officer came out onto the porch and started questioning me about what had happened. I was in no mood and I was probably a whole lot smarter than the guy who was asking the questions.

This guy had it in his head that someone had broken in and killed him. Hooey! For starters, there was Cracker and Jack, so there was no way that anyone could approach the house without the dogs sounding the alarm. Jack was so sensitive to faces that he would throw a fit when I would come over on my motorcycle with a full-face helmet on so that he couldn't see my face. He was fine as soon as I took the helmet off, but he would go nuts the minute I put the helmet on as if I had turned in to some other creature.

I also pointed out to the officer that if he bothered to look (I later found out that he already had) he would find that Josh had somewhere around fifteen guns—handguns, rifles, and shotguns—and was completely capable of defending himself.

He pointed out that the gun was on the floor and

I pointed out that I had placed the gun on the floor after I had taken it away from him.

The cop asked "Why?"

I said "Why do you think WHY? I have just found my brother with a big hole in his head and I see the gun as being the cause of the injury. I wanted to get that gun away from him so that he couldn't get hurt further! What would you have done?"

Maybe he believed me, maybe he didn't. I didn't really care. I had other things to worry about.

My, then, wife showed up and the cops finally decided to let me go—for now! Assholes!

Apparently, Josh had been upset about something. We never found out what. Supposedly, someone had seen him talking to an unknown man in the driveway earlier in the day. We never found out who it was or what had been said.

I packed him up and took him back to Parrott, and buried him with Grampa and Granny, and, later, my mother.

If you know where to look, you can still see examples of his work around the Dallas-Fort Worth area. I had more in common with him than any other sibling, full or half.

The Maids

As in many Southern families, Mama's family always had maids. The first maid, that I remember, was a woman named Bell. Bell was our maid when we first moved to Columbus. She lived in Cusseta, 18 miles away. In fact, Bell stopped being our maid when it had just gotten to be too much for Mama to make the drive to pick her up and then take her home at the end of the day. I don't remember much about her other than her name and that it had pained Mama to have to let her go. I don't remember Bell's last name.

Dixie Campbell was the next, and last, maid who worked for Mama. Dixie was there even after my brother and I had gone to live with my father's family. In many ways, Dixie was my Mama's best friend. To Mama, Dixie was just another one of God's children. To Mama, Dixie was colorless. She was a true friend to Mama and always supportive. I don't think that she understood Mama's illness, but I think she knew that Mama wasn't crazy.

Dixie was a classic. Dixie's one bad habit, in Mama's opinion, was that she dipped snuff. Mama wasn't happy about it, but she tolerated it and even bought her snuff when she went to the grocery store. Dixie was a short, stout woman. She had diabetes and her legs and feet would often be swollen and painful. Even with her health problems, I do not remember Dixie ever taking a day off due to illness.

Dixie had one unusual practice that I had never heard of before, or since. Once a year, Dixie would bring dinner for us from her house. I looked forward to these dinners. Guaranteed you were going to get some good home cooking and it would all be topped off with pickled peaches.

Dixie was not a disciplinarian. That was not her job. What she would do was point out to you that you knew you were doing something you shouldn't in such away that you would want to stop whatever it was. It was sort of like the guy who can tell you to go to hell in such a way that you will look forward to the trip. Furthermore, you were told that you knew how your Mama would feel about what you were doing, and what she would do if she was there, or when she found out. She would do it in such a way that you were shamed into behaving.

Dixie's health problems finally forced her to stop working and she moved to Alabama to live with her daughter. I do remember that Mama made the trip several years later to go see Dixie one last time before she passed. My Mama loved that woman and Dixie loved my Mama and my brother and me.

Annie Patterson was Granny and Grampa's maid, and later, helped Mama when she moved to the farm after Granny went to the nursing home. Annie replaced the maid that had been with my grandparents when Mama was little. That maid was named Partheenie and she, like the others, eventually left to go live with her children when she couldn't work anymore.

Annie was a large woman, probably a good foot, or more, taller than Dixie. She worked for Granny and Grampa much of Mama's life, and remained in her house on the farm long after she had stopped working. Mama went to visit her regularly after she went to the nursing home, sneaking her a box of snuff when the nurses weren't looking.

Annie was one tough woman. She had to be to have put up with Granny's poor treatment for all those years. Annie was a study in patience. I never saw this woman get upset the whole time I knew her, in spite of all the times that Granny gave her plenty of reason to be upset. Granny had an irritating habit of laughing at you, supposedly for being so dumb, after she had pointed out where you had gone wrong. I think that Annie had seen the result of arguing with the landlord and knew that there was nothing to be gained from complaining about her treatment. She had grown up in a time when complaining might very well get you kicked out.

Josh knew Annie better than I did because he had grown up around her. She loved "Mr. Joshua". She loved all "the babies". One of the last times I saw Annie at her house down in "The Quarter" I was probably 30 and had a handlebar moustache and beard. The first thing out of her mouth, once she figured out that it was me, was, "What's all dat stuff on yo face? Mr. Van! You need to shave that off! You is a good lookin' man and you need to get shed of dat!" She always spoke her mind, but there was no further mention after her opinion had been made known.

Some of the most important people in my childhood, the ones who made it possible to make it through all of Mama's ups and downs that I thought were normal, were the unchanging ones—the maids. They were comforters, counselors, helpers, and sometimes hiding places.

When I was a small child, playing on the farm, I knew I had a guaranteed hiding place if I could make it to the kitchen, because Annie was so big that you could easily remain out of sight if you could just get behind her enormous person and do the dance of matching her footsteps so that you remained hidden behind her. I have even hidden from Granny, who was in the same kitchen, by carefully matching Annie's footsteps, remaining behind her. Annie would just smile. She would never give me away, and if I was caught, she would just say "I didn't see you dair Mr. Van!", as if she had no idea that you were behind her.

THE "QUARTER"

When I was a child I grew up hearing the group of houses down back behind the farmhouse where the workers lived referred to as "The Quarter".

Huh?

It was actually "The Quarters", as in "the servants' quarters", but I somehow missed the "s" at the end. It was probably a silent "s". Had I heard the "s" I would have understood—the term "quarters" is a common Army term and I was an Army brat. Somehow I missed it and so I grew up wondering why it was called "The Quarter", not willing to let on that I had not understood what had been said. Remember "Dreckly"?

Did they call it "The Quarter" because it was in the back quarter of the property? Maybe, but it certainly didn't take up a quarter of the property. I didn't see any connection between this place and the "quarter" coin unless they called it "The

Quarter" because that was what Granny paid the people who lived there for an hour of labor. Maybe it was like in New Orleans. I had heard of a place called "The French Quarter"; maybe it was like that. I just took it for granted that there was some reason and I wasn't going to let on that I didn't know what the reason was. I put the reason out of my mind.

I was a teenager, in Maine, before it finally dawned on me what they had been saying. It was "Quarters", as in the place where the workers were housed.

Duh!

Burning Up the Yard

When I was seven, or eight, I was fascinated by fire. I wasn't a pyromaniac, but I did like watching the flames. One afternoon, after I got home from school, I got some matches and managed to set the uphill side of the yard on fire. It was fall and the grass was in it's dried out winter brown stage. I set a small fire and watched as the flames leapt from blade to blade of the dried out grass. I extinguished the blaze, scuffed the burned blades of grass with my feet, and was able to disperse and hide the scar.

I lit another patch, extinguished it, and then lit another, and before I knew it the fire had spread to a broad area on the upslope of the yard. Fortunately, I had two things going for me. One, is that the uphill side of our yard cut through the water table and so the ground was always soggy just below the grass. Second, I had filled a large jug with water and had it at the ready and this allowed me to slow the spreading fire long enough to get the hose and extinguish the fire.

When the fire was out I surveyed the damage and it was clear that I would not be able to conceal this. It was too big, probably an area 10 or 12 feet long, and 8 or so feet wide. I was definitely in trouble. Serious trouble. I was going to get a whippin' over this.

What to do?

Ding!

I reasoned in my seven-year-old mind that if I punished myself I could, possibly, lessen the punishment that I was going to receive as soon as Mama got home from work. I got the "whippin'" belt and proceeded to "whip" myself. This was not baby taps; it was true self-flagellation. It left marks and it hurt and, in the end, unfortunately, it did not benefit me.

When Mama arrived, it took less than the blink of an eye for her to notice the large blackened area of the yard. And she knew that I was responsible. I rushed to the car and explained that punishment would not be necessary since I had already taken care of that for her. She didn't buy it.

There is a Southern phrase that is used to describe a beating. The phrase doesn't make much sense, but it is commonly used. She said "I'm going to tan your hide!" And she certainly gave it a good effort.

That was the last time in my childhood that I set fire to anything that wasn't in a fireplace or grill, or in someway contained. Unless it was a firecracker!

It is funny to me that years later, when I was living in Maine with my father's family, my father and all of the family, except for my stepmother's mother, Gramma McCabe, and me, had gone on some sort of outing for a couple of days.

Among my father's parting instructions were that I was not to use the stove while they were gone.

My father was concerned that I would leave the stove on and burn down the house even though I had been cooking on a gas stove, with fire, ever since I could reach the top of the stove while standing on a chair, but then again he wasn't around to see that. I was also quite mobile in spite of his efforts to limit me. My father wouldn't let me get my driver's license because he was afraid I would take one of the cars and run away from home, which may have been true, but we'll never know.

Not to be slowed down by this impediment, I got involved in the blossoming touring, 10-speed bicycle craze. I worked, sometimes seven days a week, at an ice cream and sandwich shop in neighboring Lewiston. It was seven miles one-way, and I made the trip at least several times every week, in all 12 months of the year.

So I had three things that spelled disaster for me. I was mobile, I had money (from my job), and I had an attitude.

Early on the day that my father and the family were supposed to return, I pedaled down to the local lobsterman's house, and went around to the back porch, where he had a large, horizontal freezer chest that he had converted into a saltwater holding tank for his lobsters. I picked a lobster that was around two pounds. The guy charged $1 a pound.

I took the lobster home, and as I heated the water Gramma McCabe admonished me, saying that I knew that I had been told not to use the stove. I ignored her. She had a bark, but no bite whatsoever. The lobster cooked up quickly and, just as quickly, was consumed.

As I was headed back to the sink to clean up the evidence, I heard the car in the driveway. Oh S**t!

There was no masking the smell of lobster boiled in brine, and my father immediately identified the source. He screamed at me for a while and finally had to admit that all was OK, if only to himself. Can you imagine if he had known about burning up the yard? I probably should have told him about it.

Maurice

Maurice (pronounced "Maur-iss" in Georgian) was several years younger than me, and lived up and across the street from me. He lived with his mother and his sister, Sue. His mother was another single mom like my mother, but the similarity ended there. Maurice's mother worked somewhere in downtown Columbus. She dressed sharply and drove what my mother termed a "fancy" car. Sue was my age and was as "upity" as her mother. I think that their mother was "fishing" for a new husband, but never succeeded, to my knowledge, at least not while I was living in Columbus.

Not too surprisingly, I ran into Sue after I graduated from high school and came back to Georgia. She was doing the "club scene" in Columbus and doing a pretty good imitation of her mother—"fishing" for a "sugar daddy". Best as I could tell she had scoped out the field pretty well and had targeted a select few of the affluent young men. There weren't but four or five from which to choose.

We lived on the side of a very long (or so it seemed at the time) hill. Most yards had a retaining wall to separate the downhill yard from the uphill yard. The retaining walls ran out to the street and most had their mailboxes at the end of the wall closest to the street.

Now, this is before integrated steering wheel and ignition locks were common so the cars could be shifted out of gear without needing a key.

One afternoon, Maurice decided he was going to play "driving the car", so he climbed into the driver's seat of his mother's "fancy" car. After "steering" for a while, making car noises as he went, Maurice remembered that his mother moved the column shift lever when she drove, so Maurice grabbed the shift lever and shifted the car out of park.

Much to Maurice's horror, the car slowly started to move. Maurice had not planned an escape route and this was not San Francisco where people know to turn their wheels so that the car pins against the curb if the car moves. There weren't any curbs to park against anyway. So with much of the neighborhood watching in amazement, Maurice headed down the hill, visibly terrified inside the car.

Now, Maurice's house was just downhill from the crest of the hill so the roll started off slowly. There was no retaining wall between Mrs. Santini's house and Maurice's house, but there was a mailbox.

As the car gained momentum, suddenly there was a loud "Boom!" There went Mrs. Santini's mailbox. A few seconds later there was another "Boom!" There went the Daniels' mailbox and the end of their retaining wall. A few seconds later there was another "Boom!" There went the Daniels' downhill neighbors' mailbox and retaining wall. A few more seconds and "Boom!" There went the next mailbox and retaining wall. The car finally came to a stop as it got to the place where the slope of the hill flattened.

When all was said and done, Maurice had taken out four mailboxes and three retaining walls before the car finally came to rest.

The neighbors all rushed to the car where they found Maurice safe and sound. Maurice's mother was so happy to find Maurice alive that I don't believe she even punished him.

Maurice never played "driving the car" again. At least not until he was older and actually understood how driving worked.

The Bat Cave

When I was eight or nine, the original Batman movie came out. It was based on the Batman TV show that was so far fetched that the government of Mexico refused to let it be shown in that country because it was so idiotic.

Columbus was a special place, as far as the Batman movie went, because Terry Johns, of Terry Johns Motor Sports, had built the Bat Boat that they used in the movie.

My brother and I were glued to the set whenever the Batman TV show was on. We were so "into" the show that we emptied out the upper shelf of the closet that was in the TV room (there was only ever one TV in our house) and created our own Bat Cave up on the shelf in the closet.

By moving the TV out into the room a few inches, we could see the TV, although at a very acute angle, from the upper shelf in the closet. It was extremely cramped and only one of us could fit at a time, and when you were up on the shelf you could defend the position until your bladder commanded retreat.

Mama took it all in stride, sitting there, grading papers, as we took turns in the small, cramped space. Mama said "You don't have any room up there!"

"You're not supposed to have room in a Bat Cave!" we said.

Mrs. Nall

Mrs. Nall was my third grade teacher. She was also a woman who had roomed with Mama at Bessie Tiff's boarding house when she was at the University of Georgia. For anyone whose parent is a teacher, you know that the worst teacher to have is one who knows your teacher parent. Mrs. Nall was not at all above calling Mama if she had a problem with me and I knew it. Consequently, I was probably better behaved in third grade than I was the rest of my elementary school days, maybe the rest of my school days—period!

Having a teacher who knows your Mama is one thing, but having one who used to live with your Mama is another matter altogether. It's like having two Mamas. Mama gave Mrs. Nall "carte blanche".

Third grade was also an unusual year in that we saw several things that we had never encountered before. One was a student named Marquita, whose father was in the Army and who was from South, or Central, America. She spoke Spanish. Only Spanish. This is long before bilingual education and the school had told Mrs. Nall to do the best she could.

Another class member was a boy who was at least twice as big as any other kid in the class who, literally, brought his lunch to school in a suitcase like Jethro Bodean in "The Beverly Hillbillies". He had moved around so much with his military family that he was probably a couple of years older than the rest of us.

I can't remember the guy's name, but I do remember "Show and Tell" day when he brought, for his item, a real bazooka. This is a long tubular device intended to launch a sort of rocket against tanks and other armored targets. Apparently, his father was in Anti-Armor, or a tank killer, and he had given his son the bazooka to show him what Daddy did for a living. Fortunately, he had not given his son any bazooka rounds to go along with the bazooka.

Not sure what ever happened to "Bazooka Boy", but I'm sure he made out fine even if he didn't get out of elementary school until he was fourteen or fifteen.

Libraries and Museums

My mother was committed. Her sons would all get a college education if she had anything to say about it. To this end, my mother started taking us to the Bradley Memorial Library and Museum from the time that we moved to Columbus. These were places that most of my friends never knew existed.

The Bradley Memorial Library is a place of learning and beauty. The grounds are a collection of plants, exotic and beautiful, with a small, lily pad choked pond with a bridge crossing over.

We always took a slice of bread, crammed in a pocket, to feed the fish. When I was older, I once took a piece of fishing line and a hook, and caught fish as fast as I could bait the hook and toss the line, until I was out of bread. I released all of the fish (I had to. It's hard to walk with live fish in your pockets), but it was a fun and frantic time.

The Bradley Memorial Library is where I started

reading manuals, which later led to my profession as a scientist, sort of. I had just begun my lifelong interest in all things mechanical—especially motorcycles. The Bradley had an excellent collection of motorcycle service manuals for almost every kind of motorcycle you could imagine and some you couldn't. Ever heard of a Munch Mammoth? It was a BIG motorcycle made in the 60's that easily dwarfs most motorcycles made before or since. They had a manual for it.

I studied these manuals until I had practically memorized the contents of most of them. I knew about motorcycles that I would never see. I knew the manufacturers, I knew the models, and I knew who was successful in racing and who wasn't, in all different forms of racing.

There is also a Bradley Museum that is located adjacent to the library. The museum has an outstanding collection of firearms and I spent many hours there as well, studying the old and the shiny. Many of the weapons that they had were ones that I had either seen or fired. I started shooting when I was six.

The museum also houses items from the Indian tribes that once populated the region, which was another area of interest to me.

I have to credit Mama with my interest in science. Never has a mother so encouraged a child as my Mama did with my interests in nature and science. She gave us two sets of World Book Encyclopedias, a second set when she determined that the set we had was "behind the times", and when we came to her with questions the first response was usually "Look it up!"

I did not fully appreciate her approach as a child and a young man, but I appreciate it now.

Skateboards

X Games, schmeck games. When I was a kid, we got street skates one year. You know, the ones with the key that were made entirely of metal except for the leather ankle straps. Even the wheels were metal. We got a pair once a year for the next few years. The skates only lasted around nine or ten months before they were completely destroyed due to our extreme use. At that age we used them as sort of all-terrain shoes since you could walk through a couple of inches of water or mud with them on because you were raised up out of the muck by the height of the skates. This, unfortunately, does nothing good for the skates. The bearings just didn't stand up.

Many of these skates became parts of hill racers. A hill racer looks sort of like an "H" (imagine the "H" moving right to left across the page), with the legs having wheels at the ends. The rear leg is fixed to the center leg and the front leg is hinged in the middle so that the racer can be steered either by a foot on either side of the front leg or by a rope attached to the ends of the front leg. We built a lot of these. Several every year for several years. Sort of a "wooden GM".

One year, after skating all over the neighborhood for a couple of months, and before the hill racer season formally began, we heard about a thing in California called a "skateboard". We had to have one! Even though we hadn't ever seen one, we thought we got the picture. Somebody said it was like a surfboard on wheels. So, out came the hammers, nails, and tools and the skates came apart into two "trucks" per skate. A "truck" is one set of wheels—front or back. We nailed the trucks to the bottom of a board and "Voila!", pronounced "Wa La" in Georgian, we had a skateboard.

Now, there were a lot of kids in the neighborhood—Corey, Chick, and Mary Frankel, the San Peso kids (they were Filipino), Charles, and assorted other kids. What we needed was a bigger skateboard.

We got a board from a packing crate (guess where we got it?) that was roughly 16 inches wide and 8 feet long. We took two pairs of skates and built a skateboard big enough for most of the neighborhood kids, at the same time. The only problem was that we weren't engineers and didn't understand the problems inherent in the design of multi-wheel vehicles. So the skateboard did not steer well, and, in fact, we wrecked it the first time we loaded it up with six kids and probably ended, forever, several of those kids' association with skateboards.

What was needed, we thought, was a cab to provide protection in a rollover. So we commandeered a couple of orange crates from behind the local Piggly Wiggly (yes, that is a real name) grocery store, and constructed a cab complete with "seat ropes", a variation on seat belts, which were also new at the time. We had specially chosen the crates for their large, brightly colored stickers depicting the contents being harvested in some far off land.

What I didn't understand was that the cab and seat belts would only make things worse because when you crashed you would not be thrown clear. You would instead remain with the wreckage. Through the wreck. Live and learn.

The first and only time I ever drove the "cab board", I made it roughly half the way down the hill before it veered off into the yard four houses down and rolled several times with me inside.

The “cab board” was trash. I fished myself out of the “seat ropes”, stood up with part of the crate still entangling me, and declared the experiment suspended.

It wasn’t the dumbest thing I ever did (I once stood in our top loading washing machine and turned it on spin to see if I could “ride” it—no!), but it was definitely lacking in terms of thinking the problem through.

My First Ticket

I got my first ticket when I was twelve years old, sort of. I was visiting Mama, back from Connecticut by myself, and we were on our way to Parrott. We were on the other side of Richland, about the halfway point, and I had been nagging Mama to let me drive.

Mama had let my brother and me start driving in the driveway when he was 12 and I was 11. She was in a depressive phase and couldn't argue with us (I never said we were angels). It seemed harmless enough—backing down the driveway and then pulling back forward under the carport. We did this for hours.

On the way to the farm, I nagged and nagged until Mama finally gave in. She was probably on the verge of a depressive phase. She gave in and I got behind the wheel.

Now, as I have said, I was small and so I could

just see over the dash, and this was not lost on the Georgia State Trooper who had someone stopped by the side of the road when we passed.

A couple of minutes later, the Trooper appeared in the rear window with his lights flashing.

We had seen the Trooper, and Mama and I had since switched back so that she was driving when he caught up to us. I saw the Trooper and he saw us.

Mama and I discussed whether or not the Trooper wanted us to stop or just get out of his way.

Mama moved to the shoulder and, rolling down the window, motioned the Trooper past. He wasn't buying it.

Eventually Mama pulled over and, in a distraught fit of tears, began to tell the Trooper of her hard plight in life. The Trooper was obviously at a loss for what to do, and finally settled on citing her for driving without a license instead of me.

That weekend we made the run over to Cuthbert to see "Annie" and stopped in Lumpkin, where the State Troopers' office was, on the way home so that Mama could pay the ticket.

It was one of the worst things I think I ever did to her and I never asked her to drive again. Unless we were on a dirt road.

J.C. Pinkston's Name

Years later, when I was eighteen or nineteen, I went back to the farm to visit. While I was there I took mother's car and headed down toward the family ponds.

While leaving one of the ponds I managed to get the car stuck in the sandy soil. I did what I could to "un-stick" the car, but to no avail.

Within the hour an old man came by on a tractor.

I said "Hey! I'm stuck!"

He said, "I see that!" Never slowing the tractor.

"Can you help me?" I said.

"Nope!" he said.

Frustrated, I said, "I'm J.C. Pinkston's grandson!"

"Why didn't you say so!" he said.

The farmer stopped, hooked a chain to mother's car and pulled me out of the sand.

I never saw this man again, and I have no idea

who he was, but he knew who J.C. Pinkston was, and that was enough to get me unstuck.

Tree Houses

At some point when I was ten, the neighborhood gang refocused their attention to "arboreal architecture". The "hang out" spot had shifted down Matilda Lane to the house of a kid who had moved to the neighborhood. He had a Saint Bernard. It was not that it was so unusual to see a Saint Bernard in Georgia, even though it was. What was unusual was that the kid had a saddle for the dog!

The kid who had the dog was a small boy a year or two younger than us and he was small enough that he could ride the dog like a small horse. The lack of a bridle meant that the dog would only make it a few steps before the kid would fall off. Undeterred, the kid would hop back up, jump back on the dog, and they would be off again.

Now at the back of this kid's yard there was a large, old, oak tree. The large lot behind the house was the home of Burnham Van Lines, a local trucking and moving company, and there was a huge stockpile of large, heavy-duty packing crates. When I say large, I mean large like eight feet by four feet by four feet.

Over the course of that summer we removed at least five of these packing crates and hoisted them into the oak tree. By the time we were finished we had built a three or four story tree house that had enough room to house the lot of us, as many as nine or ten of us. I would guess that we went through fifty pounds of nails assembling our mansion.

The tree house was still standing when I left Georgia to go live with my father's family in Connecticut.

When I returned from Connecticut a year later the tree house was gone. According to my childhood friend Charles, the manager of the Burnham Van Lines operation had finally noticed the tree house and they retrieved their crates worried they would end up liable for an injury caused by one of their crates falling out of the tree and onto someone.

A Week's Worth of Switches

Whenever we went to the farm the last thing that happened before we left on our way either on to Cuthbert, or back to Columbus, was that Grampa would walk us out to the car, detouring by his Impala parked in the garage. He would go to the trunk, open it, and retrieve a bundle of Chinaberry "switches" (limbs used to warm our bottoms when we were bad). He had cut them and trimmed the small branches off so that they looked like small wooden horse whips.

Grampa would bring the switches to Mama and say, "Here's some switches for next week". He knew full well that she would probably exhaust the bundle before our return and she many times did. Not that my brother and I were all so bad, but Mama was not above prodding us to step up the pace if needed with a "gentle" nudge from a Chinaberry switch.

A couple of times I took the bundle and hid it after we got home, but to no avail—Grampa had an endless supply of stock.

"Spare the rod and spoil the child!" I grew up with this saying. I am not sure I really understood what it meant when I was growing up, but I did understand it had something to do with it being a good thing to switch your kids when they were "bad". I didn't understand it, but I knew that a lot of people thought it was a good idea.

"ANNIE" AND UNCLE JASPER

Most weekends when we went to the farm mother would go back to Columbus by way of Cuthbert. This involved driving on from Parrott to Dawson and then cutting across to Cuthbert and then back to Columbus by way of Lumpkin. Cuthbert was a big deal because it had the hospital. My great aunt Alva, "Annie" in our pronunciation of "Auntie", lived in Cuthbert and died in that hospital.

The one thing that made this trip tolerable to me was that there was a filling station in Cuthbert, on the square, that had live rattlesnakes. BIG, LIVE, RATTLESNAKES. It made it all worthwhile to me.

Cuthbert is also the home of Andrews College. The last time I stopped there, a past president of the college was living in "Annie's" house. He had bought it and restored it back to all its glory after he retired from the college.

Alva Hatcher lived in this large Victorian

gingerbread house. The house was originally built by a Jewish dentist shortly after Civil War times. It had the first indoor, copper bathtub in the county, it was also the house where, what would later be called Royal Crown, originally Chero-Cola, was invented by another relative.

The house is just on the edge of downtown Cuthbert, toward the college. There is a huge magnolia tree to the left and the house has several attached apartments in the rear. There was a large, overgrown lot in the rear that was chest high in weeds (for a short kid) when I was a kid.

"Annie" was an agoraphobic to the worst possible extent, even though agoraphobia was not a term that anybody had heard back then except maybe in the clinical world. She lived in three rooms of this enormous house. Her bedroom, the kitchen, and one of the bathrooms. The trip to the kitchen required that you exit her bedroom, at the front of the house, sealed from the outside world by sheets of newspaper that covered all windows except one that was in the side bay window looking out at the large magnolia, off the side of her bedroom, opposite the door.

From there you passed the two landing, mahogany staircase that took you to the second floor. Down the long hallway, beneath the final flight of stairs, you turned right, into the main dining room. The table in this room would easily seat 14 and was covered with an old, dingy tablecloth. On the table was a box of "Life" cereal that "Annie" had for breakfast every morning.

Through the dining room, past the enormous table, you turned left into the kitchen that was surprisingly small given the size of the dining room and the number of persons it was set up to accommodate.

The only other part of the house where "Annie" went was the bathroom that was closest to her bedroom. This bathroom was one room away towards the rear of the house. Normally, on those most unfortunate times that we went by "Annie's" on Saturday, we would have to stay overnight.

There were two beds in "Annie's" bedroom. My brother and I slept in one and Mama and "Annie" slept in the other. In later years, he and I got to sleep in the room on the other side of the bathroom. After we moved into the other room, Mama slept in one bed and "Annie" in the other in her bedroom. More on this other room later...

There was an ancient carpet in "Annie's" bedroom, on the side of her bed that was farthest from the door and closest to the dresser. On the dresser was a picture of a haggard looking old man. It was Uncle Jasper, "Annie's" brother. He had been injured in World War I and when he got home he was attended to by the only local surgeon. Supposedly, the doctor had done something that resulted in constant pain for Uncle Jasper although the doctor denied that there was any unresolved medical problem. As one who suffers from chronic pain I can only imagine what it would have been like for Uncle Jasper.

By the time of his death it is my understanding that he was probably addicted to morphine, which had been given to him by the doctor who said nothing was wrong.

One morning, long before I was born, Uncle Jasper woke up and asked "Annie" to get him some breakfast. "Annie" later said that he seemed at peace that morning. Often suicide victims are very calm right before the end, after they have made the decision. At that point the path is clear, the steps are determined.

"Annie" made her way to the kitchen.

Apparently, Uncle Jasper sat up, facing the large mirror on the dresser, drew a pistol from some hidden place, placed the barrel to his temple, and pulled the trigger.

"Annie" heard the report and came running from the kitchen to find Uncle Jasper, lying on the floor, dying.

Uncle Jasper died there by the side of the bed. A large brown stain, left by the blood that, no doubt, had spouted from his wound, marked the point.

"Annie" never removed the rug. She never had it cleaned either. I grew up seeing that stain every time we went to see her. We would point and say, "That's where Uncle Jasper shot his self!"

As an adult, I once stopped by the house on my way through the area. I went to the door and rang the old door ringer that, unlike the old, black, grungy ringer I remembered, was now polished silver.

I introduced myself to the person who answered the door and received a sort of "Huh?" I told the gentleman that I was the grandnephew of Alva Hatcher and he said "Why didn't you say so?" and invited me in.

The house is now restored to its late 19th century glory. Turns out the ringer and all of the door hinges in the house are silver.

The house was originally built by a Jewish dentist. The house actually has what is referred to as a "Synagogue Room". In the time that the house was built, there were very few Jewish people in the

South, so a rabbi would travel from town to town having small services with one or more families on an irregular basis.

At some point, the relative who invented Chero-Cola, later known as Nehi, later known as Royal Crown, lived in the house. Apparently a pharmacist, he formulated Chero-Cola at about the same time that Coca-Cola (the Coca-Cola that actually had cocaine in the ingredients) was getting big. I was told that Coca-Cola sued for the exclusive rights to use the word "cola".

Coca-Cola had a lot more money than Chero-Cola and in the end, even though they had won, Chero-Cola almost folded. The company responded with the introduction of Nehi during World War II (It's "knee high"!). Chero-Cola became Nehi and introduced the first tall soft drink bottles that were advertised with posters showing a young woman's leg from the knee down and the top of the bottle was level with the top of the woman's knee.

The current resident had collected and preserved a collection of Chero-Cola and Nehi memorabilia that was recovered during restoration of the house, much of which was found inside of the walls of the house. I'm not sure exactly how that stuff got there, but that is where they found it.

Alva had three sisters and the brother: Jasper who was long since dead, Janie Mae (Granny), Lila, and Maida (the only sane person in the lot and the one who died earliest). When she died, the sisters, mainly Granny and Aunt Lila, decided they could "clean up" selling the antiques in Alva's house and they sold most of the contents to an antique dealer in Albany, because you know that a dealer from Albany is serious, being from a big city like Albany and all.

About a week after they had sold off the bulk of the furnishings they were out looking at what they could now get for themselves given the windfall they had received from the sale of Alva's furniture. Oddly enough, they started seeing furniture items similar to what they had just sold to the dealer going for several times what they had gotten for their pieces. They hurried back to the dealer as fast as their little legs would carry them.

Upon their arrival, they asked the dealer for the return of their sister's items, saying they had been so distraught that they had made an error in judgment. The dealer agreed with them, saying that they had also made one other error in judgment if they thought that he was going to sell them back the items for what he had paid for them.

Between the three of them, I think they bought back a couple of items each, and ended up paying most of what they made off the sale of the items to the dealer to buy back the few pieces that they ended up with.

As I stood in the front bedroom that was "Annie's" bedroom, I asked the owner if he was aware that someone had once died in that room? He said "No."

Later in life, when I was working for the Army on a project at Fort Knox, I was at the Armor Museum and I saw the wagon that had been Patton's command center. In the command center was Patton's grandfather's sword and the bloody shirt that he was wearing when he died. These items were given to Patton when he was a young boy to remind him of his grandfather's gallantry and heroism. Southerners can be a little twisted about the past, especially when it comes to past battles.

I am not sure what the effect was on Patton, but I can guess. I can imagine the impact on the young boy who was given the bloody garment and the sword. I am thankful that I was never given anything but the stories about Uncle Jasper.

L.J.J.J.B.B.D. Hatcher

In the bedroom on the other side of the bathroom from "Annie's" bedroom there was a picture of an imposing Southern gentleman with a long, full beard. The man could have been passed off as General Thomas J. Jackson—"Stonewall". I was told that the man's name was Leon Jefferson Jackson Johnston Beauregard Batteau Davis Hatcher. He was supposedly named for every Confederate General who served in Georgia during the war.

It's funny what you remember.

The Devil Is in the Cemetery

One time when my brother and I were stuck in Cuthbert with nothing to do, we decided to go exploring in a new direction. We must have been six and seven. This was about the time that Uncle Dave and Aunt Lila had sold the two-story hotel they had owned in downtown Cuthbert where we used to be able to hang out.

We only saw Uncle Dave rarely after that and, apparently, so did Aunt Lila. After they sold the hotel, Uncle Dave became a traveling salesman. He had this large black car and whenever we did see him he always had these excellent pineapple candies that he said he got in Florida.

This day my brother and I made our way to the square and headed out of downtown on the road heading south. The square in downtown Cuthbert has roads converging from all corners, north, south, east, and west. North takes you to

Columbus, East takes you back to Dawson and the farm, and West takes you to "Annie's" house and Andrews College. Not sure where South takes you, at least I wasn't when I was six.

The South road heads out of downtown and past a cemetery. The cemetery is separated from the road by a wall such that you cannot see over into the cemetery as you pass—at least not when you are six. My brother and I passed the cemetery and, after a while, finally turned around and headed back—nothing down that way!

When we got back to "Annie's", Mama asked where we had gone, and we told her that we had gone to the square and then headed out of town past the cemetery. Mama then sat us down and told us the story of a young sharecropper's child who was walking home late one night, and as he passed the cemetery he heard voices coming from the other side of the wall saying, "One for you, and one for me, one for you and one for me".

The child, being a true believer, instantly determined that what he was hearing was the Devil and God dividing up the dead people in the cemetery! What he was actually hearing was two boys that had stolen a bunch of pecans and were dividing them up on the other side of the wall.

AAAAAAAaaaaaaaaaaaahhhhhhhhhhhhhhhh!

It was probably really funny in the 40's when it happened.

Ice Cream for Lunch

When Josh finally got married after he graduated from Auburn, Grampa would not go. I am almost positive that he knew about the supposed tryst involving his employer. Anyway, he said that he wasn't going to any weddings or funerals. This left the door open for me—if Grampa didn't have to go then maybe I didn't have to go. I have held that position myself except for a few exceptions like when I had to bury my mother, and brother, and my nephew, after he hanged himself.

Sure enough, I successfully lobbied for, and won, with Grampa's support, an exemption from going to Atlanta to the wedding. Nate went to the wedding. He was already turning into the "clothes horse" that he later became and for him it was a chance to "dress up". For me it was the possibility for mischief.

In the end there wasn't too much mischief, although Grampa and I did come across what was apparently a very large snake, while we were fishing. We got very close in to the bank and there was some very heavy animal that seemed to be slithering its way to the water and toward us. It may have been a turtle, but it would have had to be a very large turtle to cover that amount of ground as quickly as this thing did.

Anyway, we messed around at the pond until around lunch time and then we headed back to the farm. We stopped in town for the surprise.

I went into the store with Grampa and we walked back toward the two open refrigerated cases.

Huh? I thought.

Grampa retrieved a half gallon of vanilla ice cream—the kind that came in a sort of "brick".

"Lunch?" I said.

"Yep." he said.

"ALL RIGHT!" I said.

Grampa and I had a half gallon of vanilla ice cream for lunch that day. We would look at each other and chuckle from time to time as we ate the ice cream. When we couldn't hold it in any longer, thinking about what Granny would have done if she had known about this breach of the rules, we broke out laughing.

I think Grampa truly enjoyed this. I know I did!

Mrs. Santini

A short time after we moved to Columbus a family from New Jersey (i.e., "Yankees") moved in across the street. This was a loud family, like you imagine yelling from building to building in "A Streetcar Named Desire". Mama was somewhat "blind" to the misbehavings of others. I think that she believed that as soon as they found Jesus they would "straighten up and fly right", as she would say. The Santini family was Catholic.

Mrs. Santini was a large woman. Younger than Mama. She had shoulder length black hair and was about as Italian (that's "Eye-tal-yun" in Georgian) as they come. She had a couple of kids, younger than my brother and me. She was an enlisted man's wife and her husband was headed to Vietnam. They had moved here so that she would be near Fort Benning in case she needed anything while he was gone.

I don't remember much about her except for the night she met my Mama and me.

Mama wasn't going to rush over to "make the introductions". She was going to let her get settled in a little. She thought.

It was shortly after dark and the Santini's house was lit up in every room. There weren't any shades or curtains so you could see every move they made from across the street. They were unpacking. It was late summer, I think, and all the windows in our house were open to catch the breeze. We only had a single window unit air conditioner and cooled only one room—the one with the TV in it. We called that room the "TV room".

All of a sudden there came a blood-curdling scream from across the street. And again! It sounded like someone was killing Mrs. Santini! Mama headed for the door. She told us to stay! Yeah, right!

Mama headed across the street. I followed at a safe distance. What was she going to do, abandon her rescue attempt and take me back? We got to the Santinis' front door and, through the front living room window; we could see Mrs. Santini standing on a chair in the dining room that separated the kitchen from the living room. She was screaming at the top of her lungs, fidgeting, nearly falling from her perch on several occasions. On the floor, beneath the chair, running helter skelter around in frantic circles was a roach.

In Mrs. Santini's defense, the roaches in Georgia, especially next to woods, can get quite large. If you see one flying at night you can mistake it for a small bird or a bat (we had those too). I'm talking two inches, or longer. She was from the north, and, once you get far enough north that the ground freezes deep in the winter, you don't see too many roaches.

Mama entered the house and quickly assessed the situation, moved to the chair Mrs. Santini was standing on, and it was "Squash!" with some very low crackling noises as the roach's body was crushed beneath her shoe. No more roach running around.

After repeatedly reassuring Mrs. Santini that the roach was, in fact, dead, Mama helped her down from the chair. She helped her to the couch in the living room and got her a glass of water. Mama introduced us. Mrs. Santini skipped introducing herself. She skipped right to "What was that thing?"

Apparently, as hard as it is for anyone from the South to imagine, Mrs. Santini had never seen such a creature, and she had been literally terrified.

Mama told her not to worry and made the "squashing" motion with her foot to demonstrate the correct action to use on the little terrors. After that, Mama was at the top of the list in Mrs. Santini's book for as long as they lived across the street.

I don't remember what happened to the Santinis. I think that her husband made it back from Viet Nam and they moved back to the North Country. I do remember that Mama was glad to have someone that would listen to her. Mrs. Santini had to. Mama had saved her life!

Fish Heads on the Smokehouse

Grampa was a genuine award-winning fisherman. He had a whole handful of fishing awards from Field and Stream magazine. Almost all are for largemouth bass. I still have several of these. If I remember correctly, all of the bass awards are for fish that were greater than twelve pounds.

When I was a kid Grampa would clean the fish he had caught on the back porch. There was a long, narrow, board that was the cleaning and cutting surface. The board was around six feet long and probably fourteen to sixteen inches wide and about waist high. There was a one-inch high lip on the far and near sides, but it was open at either end. The lips helped keep the fish, or watermelon, from getting away from you and the open ends allowed you to rinse the fish guts or watermelon seeds off the board toward either end. The assorted farm cats made short work of whatever fish parts hit the ground.

After cleaning the day's catch, Grampa would take any bass head that was big enough to stick your fist in its mouth, and nail it to the smokehouse so that it looked like the heads were emerging from the wood, and take a stick and prop the mouth wide open. Sort of Southern farm-style gargoyles.

The heads actually served several purposes. Grampa would never boast. Never! So this was about as close to boasting as it came. The smokehouse was not visible from the road and in order to see the fish heads you had to be in the backyard looking "out". If you were looking "in" there was no way to see the heads. It was sort of his private trophy wall.

Another thing the fish heads did was draw all of the flies away from the kitchen. No matter how good the smell was coming from the kitchen, no fly is going to pass up a drying fish head.

Most of the fish that I caught were not big enough to merit a place on the smokehouse. I caught more bream, or what some folks call sunfish, than anything else, and bream heads don't really lend themselves to being nailed to a wall.

One afternoon while Grampa and I were fishing, I managed to "snag" a large catfish. "Snagging" is when a fish brushes against a hook, or lure, and the fisherman mistakes the "bump" for a strike and ends up "snagging" the fish with the hook when they attempt to set it.

I snagged this fish, we would later find, in the back on one side of the dorsal fin in the meatiest part of the fish's back. This is probably the least injurious place that you could ever snag a fish and it became instantly clear that he may have been hooked, but he wasn't hurt.

The place where I had snagged the fish was the perfect place to hook it if you were going to have the fish tow something and the fish proved it by pulling Grampa and me around the three-acre pond several times.

That fish fought, pulling the boat around the pond, for close to an hour. Toward the end, the fish would rest for a minute or two, or until you started trying to reel him in, and then he would take off again.

We finally landed the fish and Grampa said that because of the injury that we would not be able to release him and would have to take him home. The catfish was close to three feet in length and probably weighed close to twelve pounds. It was a young, healthy fish and not your typical fat, somewhat grotesque looking, fish that large catfish normally are.

For me, the catfish was my ticket to having a fish head on the smokehouse because this catfish's head was clearly large enough to merit a place on the fishing "Wall of Honor". I was so proud. Somewhere there is a photograph of me standing in front of the smokehouse with my fish's head nailed to the wall with the stick propping it's mouth open.

Eatin' Possum

One of the benefits of having a grandfather like Grampa was all the neat stuff you got. At one point he built us a large cage and got someone to catch us five young flying squirrels. My brother and I took them home to Columbus and we would close the bedroom door and let the squirrels out of the cage. They would scamper up the curtains and then "fly" across the room, landing on the footboard posts. Then they would scamper across the bed and back up the curtain and do it again.

Another benefit was that there was plenty of game and fresh caught fish to eat. One year my grandfather paid Bully to catch him a possum. We kept the possum in the long, now empty, flying squirrel cage for several weeks in order to both fatten him up and to make sure that he wasn't sick.

The possum was to be the feature that year for Thanksgiving dinner. When you are seven or eight on a farm in the South this is about as neat as it gets!

The possum gained several pounds during his stay on its diet of fresh peanuts. On Thanksgiving morning Grampa dispatched the possum, skinned and cleaned it, and turned it over to Granny and Annie for final preparation.

Possum tastes surprisingly like roast beef. A moist, somewhat greasy, roast beef. It was extremely tender and the meat literally fell off the bone. It was actually quite good.

For me, one of the biggest bonuses was that anytime Jed Clampett, on "The Beverly Hillbillies", talked about eating possum I could proudly say "I've eatin' possum!"

We ate a lot of strange things on the farm. The South survived the Civil War due in part to their ability to make do with what they had. A friend of mine used to tell about a barefooted, young boy that he came across, walking down a dirt road carrying a large bird of some sort. He stopped and rolled down the window and asked the boy "Say, what chu got there boy?"

"Cheek-In Hawwk!" replied the boy.

"What chu gonna do with that Cheek-In Hawwk?" my friend asked.

"I'm gonna make me some gumbo." said the boy.

"Cheek-In Hawwk make pretty good gumbo, does it?" asked my friend.

"Bout like al (owl)!" replied the boy.

BIRDEE, TOM, THE BLACK GUY, AND THE DYNAMITE

As I have said, my Aunt Birdee is different. At times, she can be real different.

She had a boyfriend named Tom, back in the 60's. Now, she was a fairly wild child. She once told me that she had been in two plane crashes, one each on two consecutive days, in airplanes piloted by the same guy. She went off to New York to be a star and ended up married to a guy that supposedly managed some famous singer for a time at some point later.

She was shortly divorced and ended up back in Parrott. Somewhere along the way, she took up with Tom, who was obviously challenged, as you will see. She and Tom took a survey of the situation and came to the conclusion that she was in line to inherit the house in Parrott and all of Aunt Addie's estate. Addie was Grampa's sister.

They determined that they could accelerate her inheritance if they got rid of Aunt Addie. Tom enlisted the help of a local black guy that supposedly knew something about dynamite and had access to dynamite. Tom was wanting to move things along as quickly as possible.

One night, they and their accomplice picked up some dynamite and blasting caps and headed to Aunt Addie's house in Parrott. Somewhere along the way, they determined, as they later said, that they had an excess of dynamite, and since Aunt Birdee and Granny had not seen "eye to eye" for years, they decided that they should go ahead and blow Granny up as well, as soon as they were done with Aunt Addie.

At some point, the trio arrived at Aunt Addie's house, only a short distance from downtown Parrott.

Now Aunt Addie's house is one of the grandest in Parrott. It was also where Aunt Birdee was living at the time (another indication that they had not really thought this through). It is a single story, Victorian-style, with a porch the traverses the front and both sides of the house. The yard is above the road by at least 18 inches and slopes sharply to the road. Apparently they had pulled up and gotten out, and opened the trunk of the car. The black man was apparently assembling the blasting caps and the sticks of dynamite when the explosives went off, blowing the black man to pieces. Fortunately for Aunt Birdee and Tom, the black man took the brunt of the blast and deflected it around them.

The two of them were blown up onto the lawn. Supposedly, their clothes were also blown off.

The Sheriff's Department showed up later. I have been told that the Deputy was somehow also a relative—distant cousin or something.

They were held accountable and Tom took the blame and I was told that he spent a time in the mental hospital. Aunt Birdee came home for an extended period of convalescence.

Granny was never really in any danger, although I wished that she had at least been scared. Aunt Birdee and Tom told the State Troopers that when they figured out that they had way more dynamite than they needed, that they had decided to blow up Granny as well, but of course, they never made it over to Granny's house due to the mishap at Aunt Addie's.

Daddy

My Daddy was a classic in some respects. He had lied about his age to get into the Army in World War II. He had served in the horse Cavalry up until the time it was disbanded. He had earned a Purple Heart in the South Pacific during World War II. He also served in Korea. And then the Army doctors told him he had had a heart attack. My father was given a medical discharge that he fought for some time. In the end it was determined that he had apparently had a muscle spasm. There was no evidence of a heart attack. Oh well, too late to go back now.

Before he left the Army he had ended up as the commander of a truck company. He left the Army at the rank of Captain. According to his brother Claude, who started going by "Doug" in his later life much like I was "Bill" for a year, my father could have made it farther if he had just kept his mouth shut, but that was something he couldn't do. Claude retired as a Full, or "Bird", Colonel. Once during a Strategic Air Command (SAC) exercise that involved a general who went on to be commander of U.S. Forces in Viet Nam, my father said that the only organization that had had a clue as to what was going on was the Air Force—this general was head of the Army forces in the exercise. It did not endear Daddy to the general.

He was marooned on an island in the South Pacific for several weeks during World War II. During that time he had nothing to eat except coconut. Till the day he died he did not permit coconut of any form to be brought into the house. He could not tolerate the smell of it. I guess it took him back.

When I was living with him, I once got into a discussion with one of my younger half-siblings about the chicken that we were having.

Daddy had little or no science background and he was skeptical of what he had had because of the conflicts between science and the Bible. I was encouraged in science since before I could read by Mama. With fork in hand I proceeded to "dissect" the chicken thigh. I pointed out the skin, the muscles, fat, blood vessels...

“Some of it is just flesh!” said Daddy in a stern voice.

“No! There is no such thing as “just flesh!” I said.

He didn’t pursue it, but I am sure he felt he was right. Didn’t the Bible talk of “flesh”? I think it was the thing he felt most uncomfortable about when it came to dealing with me. I think he may have been afraid that, maybe, I knew more than he did, at least when it came to science.

When I was in first grade, around Christmas time, I was summoned to the Principal’s Office. When you’re in first grade all you know about the Principal’s Office is that it is where they send you when you are in serious trouble. That was where they later sent Jack on a daily basis, mostly for smoking from the time he was nine. It was not somewhere I had ever been except when I had to go to Fort Benning to see the dentist and Mama would send a taxicab to the school to pick me up and take me out to Main Post. Those days I would wait in the office until the cab arrived.

I headed across the schoolyard; my classroom was in what was supposed to be a temporary building, but one that was still there the last time I drove past the school some 40 years later.

Tillinghurst Elementary had an impressive main

entrance and foyer (when you're six). There was a rounded ceiling and large glass double doors separating the main foyer and offices from the hall system that ran the length of the school.

Apparently, they had not coordinated for my brother and I to show up together or maybe it was part of my mother's plan to keep her children from being kidnapped. Something that we later learned that she had been concerned about. Truthfully, I do not believe that he wanted to kidnap us so much as to show his new wife what a caring father he was. One of the secretaries at the school told Mama later that there had been a woman waiting in the car that my father had come in.

I arrived at the front of the school to be greeted by a tall, imposing man. The light was behind him so that what I remember seeing was just a silhouette.

The silhouette spoke. "Do you know who I am?"

"I think you're my Daddy." I said.

He motioned to me and I ran to him and after a few hugs and a "goodbye" I was off, back to my class. My brother apparently saw him after me. Mama knew that Daddy was coming and wanted to make sure that even if he snatched one of us, he wouldn't get us both.

That was the first time I had seen my father since

I was four. I didn't see him again until I was twelve, when my brother and I arrived in Connecticut. After not having seen me since that day in the foyer at school his first comment was, "You need a haircut!"

What do you say to that?

Waylon and Madame

Parrott is a unique place. It is a small town where time is frozen in some ways. It was named for my Great, Great Uncle John Parrott. Uncle John founded the town after the Civil War. He had fought at both battles of Bull Run, which is no small feat. Few who were at the first battle survived until the second. Grampa told me that Uncle John was shot once in the stomach, but that he was at sufficient range that the mini-ball had struck him, but had not penetrated his body.

Parrott is home to several celebrities. Joanna Moore, Tatum O'Neil's mother, is from Parrott. My cousin Jeanie's mother, Aunt Birdee, was at one point married to a guy that later managed some '70's recording star. Or so I was told. Another cousin started Cunningham Arts in Atlanta, which started the "Decoupage" craze of the 60's and 70's, before he died mysteriously in a warehouse fire. And then there is Waylon.

Waylon was a somewhat distant cousin from my Great Uncle Smedley's side of the family. If you have ever watched old reruns of "Hollywood Squares", you have probably seen Waylon. He had a hand puppet named "Madame" who could be a pretty nasty piece of work in Waylon's Las Vegas show. "Madame" was a composite of a woman named Miss Lela and Aunt Birdee.

"Madame" wore a beaded hat from the 1920's that was modeled after Ms. Lela's usual hat and wore lipstick out and about her lips like Aunt Birdee. "Madame" spoke with Aunt Birdee's voice—an excited, loud, sometimes almost scary voice. "Madame" was also as risqué as she was odd looking in Waylon's interpretation.

In the 70's the National Endowment for the Arts (I believe that was the organizing body) arranged for a collection of art from museums all over America to be loaded on a train and then the exhibit traveled across the country. They called it "The Art Train". As "The Art Train" made its way through Georgia, much to the dismay of larger, more important cities, it stopped only in Parrott. Not Albany, or Dawson, or Plains (Jimmy Carter's hometown), or Columbus, but in Parrott and only in Parrott. It may have been because Parrott has a quaint little "Petticoat

Junction"-sort of train station/depot that has been maintained for many years as a sort of museum. Or, it may have been that Parrott is just an excellent example of the prototypical small southern farm town—downtown was used as the set for a movie about Jesse James, that was filmed in the 70's.

As part of the Art Train festivities, Waylon flew in from California, or Las Vegas, or wherever he was working at the time, and put on a show for the town. Now Waylon was gay, and gay is not something you want to be in Parrott, or any rural farm community in the South, at least not back when Waylon had lived there. In fact, it would (and still will) get you killed in some communities. I did not see the show, but Josh did. He and Waylon were about the same age and both had left Parrott because it had little or nothing to offer them in terms of their artistic abilities. Josh said that it was like he let loose all of the frustration, fear, humiliation, and mistreatment that had built up inside of him over all those years. Now he was the star. Now he was the one that everyone wanted to see. My brother said he let them have it! With both barrels!

This is the Bible belt. There are two white (as in "white people", although one of the churches is actually white in color) churches in town. A

Methodist church and the Parrott Baptist church, where most of the residents that we knew went to church. Most of the residents of Parrott had probably never even heard some of the phrases that were part of the Waylon's act. The temperature in the room probably went up a few degrees during the show, based only on the amount of blushing that went on. Sort of a white Eddie Murphy act with a puppet.

So he finally got his revenge and then headed back to wherever he was working. He never made it back again. He died a few years later. Every now and then, you can catch reruns of "Hollywood Squares" and see the pair of them cracking up the audience and the other contestants. Of course he had to tone it down for TV. Knowing Aunt Birdee and the story behind "Madame", makes it even funnier to me.

Connecticut

At the end of my eleventh year mother had one of her “nervous breakdowns”. Actually just a really bad depressive cycle. My mother had met a well-to-do widower who had two identical twin daughters who were in the middle between my brother’s age and mine. The Wiggins twins. They got billed on the front page of the Arts section of the local newspaper for their roles as the king’s two daughters in a local production of “The King and I”.

Mama had only known Mrs. Wiggins for a short time so, in her defense, Mrs. Wiggins had no idea what she was getting herself into. As Mama began to crater, Mrs. Wiggins panicked and before you knew it, Mama was at Saint Mary’s Hospital in the psychiatric ward, awaiting ECT, or electro-convulsive therapy, and my brother and I were on a bus headed for New York City.

Mrs. Wiggins had arranged for us to be sent to my

father's. We were to meet up in New York City. Mama would have never done this to us. She would have at least scraped up the money for airfare so that we weren't alone on a bus late at night and across the bulk of the eastern seaboard on a trip that took two days.

The trip started out all right, but soon deteriorated. We learned that "Express Bus" means that you stop at every community that has a population larger than two cats. My brother and I both had new shoes that had not had a chance to get broken in. My brother made it. Unfortunately, after the first day, my feet were hurting so bad that I took my shoes off.

Big mistake!

That was the last time I got those shoes on for the duration of the trip. My feet had swollen to at least one size larger than when I started. The next morning we made a stop and I had to put the loafers on like slippers with the back folded down, sticking me in the heel.

And so the trip went. I never got the shoes back on and when we finally met up with my father in New York City he just looked at me and said "How come you don't have your shoes on?"

Duh! Because they are so much more

comfortable this way with this big fold of leather sticking me in the heel because I can't get my feet into them!

I survived the trip, but I have never been willing to go on a long-range bus trip ever since.

I lived in Ledyard, Connecticut for one year. I was in the seventh grade at a school that was probably the best funded public school that I ever attended.

Since I had been snatched from Georgia, with no end in sight, I decided to make the best of it. To this end I decided that I would "go with the flow". So, arriving at school on the first day I was confronted with people calling me "Bill" Harding. I also got a job throwing newspapers for a large newspaper.

Now my first name is William, but I was named after my step-grandfather who died a month before I was born and his name was William VanKeuren. He went by "Pop Van" so when I was born and named for him, I became "Van". When the people at the school referred to me as "Bill", I said to myself, "What the hell!" and I became "Bill" for one school year, part of the time.

Now we went to church in Groton, far away, and there were only a couple of kids that I went to school with who also went to the same church where they knew me as "Van". So all I had to do was to explain the situation to them and all would be cool.

It actually worked extremely well. No one ever told until the end of the year parent/teacher conferences.

My father returned that evening from the conferences and as he entered the house he bellowed for me. I had a pretty good idea what he wanted. I was no dummy.

He had been taken off guard when the teachers tried to match up who "Van" was since they knew me as "Bill".

He probably calmed down a little when he found out that I was doing pretty well regardless of the name I was using at the time. I believe I was second, or third, in the 7th grade Spelling Bee.

He wanted to know why I had let the people at the school call me "Bill" to which I replied that I didn't really care what they called me as long as I understood when they were talking to me.

During the summer, after 7th grade, my father foolishly let my brother and I return, together, to Georgia for a visit. Mama was out of the hospital and supposedly doing well. The only problem with the plan was that I had no intention of returning to Connecticut.

My brother would take no responsibility, but he wasn't going either if I wasn't going. Now, you have to understand that his dream was to play professional football, even though he never would have because he is too short. But Georgia is football country, where the high school football players trained all year long as if they were collegiate, or professional, football players. Football is serious stuff in the South. He knew that if he didn't go to school and play football in the South he would never attain his dream.

If my brother was forced to move to New England then there was no hope. It hit him pretty hard.

In the end, I won out. Mama couldn't put us on the train, plane, bus, or whatever because I would run. My father was apparently tied up with moving to Maine as part of his job so that he could not come retrieve us.

We won...for the moment.

Off to the North Country

In the end my father won, at least for a time. He came and collected us toward the end of the summer, before my freshman year in high school, and hauled us back to Maine. I got my first real, regular job the day I got there—feeding and caring for three, and later four, standard bred racehorses. I ended up doing all four years at Lisbon High School in Lisbon Falls.

Like I said, he won for a time. I was headed back to Georgia within a week of graduating from high school. Shortly before I left Maine, my father asked me if I thought I would ever see him again after I left. I said "No." It seemed to be the answer he expected.

I never did see him again, but I did talk to him one more time before he was killed in a car accident. I had decided to shift the burden from myself back to him. I told him that, while I didn't necessarily agree with his approach to child rearing, I did understand why he did what he did and told him that, if I had been in his shoes, I would have probably done the same. I hope this gave him some peace about the war that went on between us since the time I was twelve.

After arriving back in Georgia I stayed with mother for about two months until Josh came to collect me and take me off to my new life in Texas.

There are still more stories from Georgia, all the stories from Maine, more Mama stories and Josh stories, and all the stories from Texas and the West. There are also all the stories that I have remembered since I wrote this, and I remember more each day.

But that's for another book, or two, or three...

Also available from PublishAmerica

FORMULA FOR LOVE AND DESTRUCTION

by C.F. Brannum

What do a recurring dream, two burglaries, a dead detective, a closet homosexual, and five beautiful women have in common? A *Formula for Love and Destruction.* But Wanda has a secret that will leave two people dead and one seriously wounded. Into the mystery to find the missing formula, one will find love amidst mystery and murder. The story is filled with romance and spots of humor, but there is an implied battle of good versus evil, a spiritual tug-of-war, and the desire to do what is right through faith and belief in God.

Paperback, 360 pages
6″ x 9″
ISBN 1-60672-569-6

Wanda Lipscomb has a secret, and Wilhelmina Brantley has a recurring dream. They are connected, but neither woman knows how until it's discovered that the formula for a life-saving drug is missing…

About the author:

C.F. Brannum is a native of Washington, D.C. While she has written scores of poems and short stories as a hobby, *Formula for Love and Destruction* is her first serious novel. A retired marketing manager, she currently lives with her husband in Fort Washington, Maryland. They have one daughter.

Available to all bookstores nationwide.
www.publishamerica.com